JESSICA BECK
THE DONUT MYSTERIES, BOOK 53
DONUT DISTURB

The First Time Ever Published!
DONUT DISTURB
The 53rd Donut Mystery

Jessica Beck is the *New York Times* Bestselling Author of the Donut Mysteries, the Cast Iron Cooking Mysteries, the Classic Diner Mysteries, the Ghost Cat Cozy Mysteries, and more.

WHEN A MURDER HAPPENS onstage during the dress rehearsal for Max's new play, Suzanne and Grace must dig into the lives of the cast and crew to see who may have just ended the production before it could even begin.

To P,
Always and Forever.
Thank you, for everything.

Chapter 1

"THANKS FOR COMING WITH me tonight," I told my best friend, Grace Gauge, as we sat in the auditorium, waiting for the curtain to go up on the dress rehearsal for *Who Killed The Prom King?*, a play being produced and directed by my ex-husband, Max Thornburg. We had received four tickets for opening night the next evening, but since our men had left town together on a guys' bonding trip, Max had insisted that Grace and I come early to get a sneak peek of the play. It was supposedly set in a typical American high school, and in line with my ex's usual MO, the actors cast as teens were all senior citizens. As a matter of fact, the only people *under* sixty cast in the play were the parts of a teacher and the school principal, both local high school students playing against type as well. It was a murder mystery comedy, something that I thought would be extremely hard to pull off, and clearly Max was nervous about it as well.

"Are you kidding? This is the most excitement I've had in ages," Grace said as she looked around the filling auditorium.

"Seriously? You're still a newlywed," I teased her.

"I mean *this* kind of excitement," she answered with a smile. "Believe me, I've got plenty of extracurricular..."

"I'm going to stop you right there," I said as I cut her off. "I don't need the details of your personal life."

"You're right; you don't," Grace replied with a grin as she turned and waved to someone behind us. "Look, the mayor brought his arm candy."

I turned and waved to George Morris and Angelica DeAngelis. They were dressed quite a bit more nicely than Grace and I were, but on the other hand, they were on what was clearly a date, so they kind of had to be. "They are perfect for each other," I said as I smiled at them and waved.

"Really? A grumpy old ex-cop mayor and a beautiful chef? Does that honestly make sense to you, Suzanne, or have you been breathing too many fumes at that donut shop of yours?"

"I don't mean their occupations. I'm saying they both have good hearts. It's nice to see they've found each other," I said.

"You're always the romantic, aren't you?" she asked.

"Don't try to lie to me, girl; I know you too well. You're every bit as bad as I am."

Grace grinned. "Guilty as charged. You know, I'm kind of surprised there aren't more people here tonight," she added as she kept looking around.

"Remember, it's just supposed to be family, friends, and honored guests," I said.

"If that's true, why is *he* there?" she asked as she pointed to Ray Blake, the owner and only employee of the *April Springs Sentinel*, our small town's excuse for a newspaper.

"I'm guessing he's here to review the play," I said.

Ray waved to me, and after a second, I gave him a half-hearted nod back. Ray and I had been on tenuous ground ever since he'd accused me of murder. He had just been trying to get a reaction out of me at the time, and he'd gotten one, but it hadn't been the one he'd been hoping for. His stunt had also managed to get him into hot water with his daughter, Emma, my assistant at Donut Hearts, and his wife, Sharon, who helped Emma run the place the two days a week when I was off. Ever since our latest confrontation, he'd been trying to get back into my good graces, but I wasn't sure when, if ever, that was going to happen.

"Did you hear the latest from our guys? Stephen and Jake are staying another two nights in Banner Elk," I told her.

"I heard," she said with a shrug. "My husband called me the same time yours was calling you. They *claim* they don't get any cell reception at the cabin, something I think both men like, to be honest with you."

"What do you think about our guys batching it without us?" I asked her. "You're not worried about Stephen getting himself into some mischief, are you?"

"Not with Jake along to supervise, not to mention the fact that they are out there in the middle of nowhere," she said with a grin.

"To be honest with you, I don't see how much trouble they *can* get themselves into," I agreed. "I didn't even know Stephen *had* an uncle, let alone one with a cabin in the woods he was willing to loan out."

"The truth is that he and Walt have been estranged for years," Grace said. "The older man has been trying to make amends with Stephen for years, and my new husband finally relented."

"What happened that split them up in the first place?" I asked.

"I don't know. Stephen doesn't like to talk about it, so I haven't pushed him on it."

I grinned at her. "And you're going to just let him get away with *not* telling you something?"

"Trust me, I'm careful to pick my battles, and this isn't one worth having."

"Seriously though, how *is* married life treating you?" I asked her.

"It's really good. He stays at my house two nights a week, and I stay at his one. I have to admit that it's pretty perfect, actually."

"Don't you miss him on the nights you aren't together?" I asked, thinking about all of the times that Jake was away from home, working on a case. As a retired state police inspector who now worked as a police consultant, he had to take the jobs where he could find them, and most of the time, that meant he was out of town when he was working, but it made him happy, so who was I to complain?

"As a matter of fact, it makes the times we're together that much more special. I recommend our living arrangement wholeheartedly to anyone." She added after a slight pause, "Well, maybe not to you, but anyone else."

I was about to say something when the house lights dimmed into darkness.

Apparently, the play was about to begin. It was five minutes after the scheduled beginning time, but I had to figure that Max had needed a bit more to get his amateur cast ready. I was excited to see what he'd been able to come up with, but unfortunately, that was not to be, though I didn't know it quite yet.

The curtains parted to reveal an older man sitting center stage, dressed in a tuxedo, slumped over in a chair with a tinfoil crown on his head. There was a knife in his chest and a rather realistic amount of blood staining his white ruffled shirt. I had to give the playwright credit. There was no suspense as to where the title of the play had come from.

A gray-haired old woman wearing a ball gown and a matching crown came onstage and gasped audibly at the sight of her date.

"Johnny? Johnny? Oh no," she emoted rather melodramatically, and then, in a much more realistic tone, she screamed. "Hal? Hal! Are you okay?"

"I thought his name was supposed to be Johnny," Grace said softly.

"That's Hal Embry," I whispered. "She must have forgotten her next line."

On stage, the geriatric ingénue shook the prom king's shoulder, and much to my surprise, the king tumbled onto the stage, the knife now sticking prominently skyward as he landed on his back.

"Cut," Max called out as he walked onto the stage. "Celia, you called him Hal, not Johnny, and Hal, what's with the theatrics?" Max then turned to us. "Sorry, folks, but evidently we're still working out some kinks. We'll be right with you." He then studied Hal a moment before leaning down and mumbling something to himself. After shaking Hal's shoulder, Max took a closer look at the wound and the blood-stained shirt. "Dr. Hicks. We need you," he called out into the audience.

I hadn't even seen Zoey Hicks in the audience before. She was the relatively new coroner for April Springs, an attractive young doctor who had expressed more than a passing interest in Grace's husband. Tonight, she was with a man I didn't recognize, handsome and, from the look of it, quite a bit older than she was.

Though Dr. Hicks was dressed in a short, sparkly red dress, she rushed to the stage with her medical bag and leaned over Hal's body. As she checked for a pulse, I was amazed that we weren't getting more of a show than we were, based on the height of that skirt, but she somehow managed to keep the rating PG and not R, though how she did it I had no idea.

I was about to say something to Grace about what was happening right in front of us when I saw the doctor shake her head briefly and stand.

Evidently, the show was over.

For the rest of us, it was temporary, but it looked as though Hal Embry had performed his last act on stage right in front of us.

"Folks, I'm afraid this production is over. If you'll show some ID to the officers on the way out, I'd greatly appreciate it. We ask you to be patient with us while we sort this out." Darby Jones had clearly been nervous addressing the crowd of most of the VIPs in April Springs. I hadn't even realized that Stephen had left Darby in charge when he'd left.

"Darby? Seriously?" I asked Grace.

"Stephen made him his second-in-command before he left. He wants to give him more responsibility, but who would have ever believed there'd be a murder in April Springs while he and Jake were gone?"

"Are you kidding? With the history of this town, just about *any-body* should have realized that something bad was bound to happen," I told her. "I'm starting to think we're the murder capital of North Carolina, if not the South."

"You're exaggerating, and you know it. Things aren't that bad, Suzanne," she said.

"I don't know about that. They sure seem that way to me sometimes," I said as another familiar cop approached us where we stood.

"Suzanne, do you and Grace have a second?"

"Sure. What's up, Rick?" I asked him.

"Come on. I'm on duty," he said. "Show some respect."

"Sorry, Officer Handler," I said, correcting my earlier error. "We didn't do it. As a matter of fact, Grace and I never left our seats."

Officer Handler looked flustered. "Nobody ever said you did."

"Then why do you need to speak with us?" Grace asked him.

"I don't. Darby does."

"Don't you mean Officer Jones?" I asked him, tweaking him a little.

"Yeah. Right. Of course. Though it's Acting Chief Jones at the moment," he said. "Anyway, he'd like to see you both backstage."

I had no idea what the summons was about, but I wanted to get closer to the action if I could do it without making it obvious that was what I was up to. After all, I'd been involved in solving a few murders in the past, and whether I liked the fact or not, I'd gotten pretty good at it.

Darby headed us off before we could get anywhere near the body, though. Someone had closed the curtain, but I wanted to get a better look at Hal Embry and the crime scene in general. Tall and handsome with his salt-and-pepper hair and his trim build, Hal came by Donut Hearts occasionally, but I wouldn't call him a regular. I couldn't imagine why anybody would want to kill him, but I knew even less reason that the acting police chief would summon Grace and me at the start of his investigation.

"What's up, Chief?" I asked him.

Officer Jones flinched a bit as I said it. "I still can't get used to that title. Honestly, I don't want to. I don't know what Chief Grant was thinking putting me in charge, let alone making me his second-in-command when he isn't here."

"He obviously thought you could handle it, or he wouldn't have done it," Grace said. "Was he wrong?" she snapped out.

"No, ma'am," Darby said as his spine stiffened a bit.

I thought Grace was being a bit rough on him, but it wasn't the right time to say anything to her about her tone. In a softer voice than she'd just used, I asked, "What can we do for you, Darby?"

"I can't reach either *one* of your husbands," he said, clearly exasperated. "Do you have any idea why that might be?"

"The cabin they are staying in doesn't get any cell phone service," Grace told him. "We can't talk to them ourselves unless they go into town, which is a good twenty miles from where they're staying."

The acting chief clearly wasn't happy about that news. "They're still coming back in the morning though, right?"

"Sorry," I said with a frown. "They just called us an hour ago and said that they were extending their trip another few days."

Grace added, "My apologies. I meant to give you the message. Stephen said that he had so much faith in you that he's going to catch up on a bit of his vacation time."

"Okay then, that's that," he said. "I can do this," he added softly, almost as though he was telling himself and not us.

"You really can," Grace said as she put a hand on his shoulder. "We have faith in you."

"You and Suzanne, you mean?" he asked with a hint of a grin.

"Of course, but our husbands do as well," Grace said.

I wasn't exactly sure how Jake felt about the acting chief, but I decided to keep that to myself. "Absolutely," I said, doing my best to sound confident. "Is there anything *we* can do to help? We've had some luck in the past with these kinds of things, you know."

"I know you have," he said as he frowned. "I'm still not sure that I should be getting help from you, given the fact that you are a pair of civilians."

"You could always think of us as unpaid consultants, if that helps," I said. "Come on, Darby. What do you have to lose?"

"Yeah, maybe you're right," he said.

I tried to hide my surprise. I hadn't dreamed there would be a chance he'd go for that line of weak logic, but I wasn't going to blow it now.

He looked around before he spoke again. "Only not here, okay? After we finish checking out the crime scene, I'll come by the cottage." Almost as an afterthought, he added, "If it's not too late for you, Suzanne."

"Don't worry about it," I said. "I can always have Emma and Sharon come in tomorrow."

I was getting out my phone to call my assistant when Darby said, "If it's all the same to you, I'd rather you didn't. The truth is that I don't want to give *him* reason to snoop around any more than he's bound to already." The "him" he was referring to was obviously Ray Blake. Darby had a point. If I called in the newspaperman's wife and daughter to come sub for me at the last minute, Ray would know something was up for sure.

"Fine. You're right. Don't worry about the time. I'll be up."

"We'll *both* be waiting for you at Suzanne's," Grace said. "See you later, Chief."

"*We* will?" I asked Grace after we headed for the exit along with the few stragglers still at the theater, including Max.

"Of course *we*. I could use some company tonight after what we just saw, and I'm pretty sure that you can too. Besides, you'll *never* stay awake if I'm not there to keep you company," she said.

"That's probably true." I'd been planning to take a nap until Darby showed up, but hanging out with Grace would be even better. After all, I'd have plenty of time to sleep later.

Just not tonight.

Max was deep in conversation with Officer Handler by the back door when we reached the exit, and I thought we might be able to sneak by him, but there was no such luck.

"Suzanne, I need to talk to you," he said as my ex-husband excused himself from the cop.

It appeared that I wasn't going to have any choice in the matter.

Chapter 2

"I'M SO SORRY ABOUT what happened tonight," I told Max before he could say another word. "You must be devastated."

"I am, naturally," my ex said. "I can't believe someone killed one of my actors right under my nose."

"Not literally though, right?" Grace asked him icily. While I'd managed to mostly forgive my ex-husband, I couldn't always say the same for my best friend's attitude when it came to Max.

"Of course not," he said tersely before turning back to me. "The truth of the matter is that I need your help, Suzanne."

"What did you have in mind?" I asked him, though I had a sneaking suspicion where this conversation was heading.

"You need to figure out who did this," Max said softly, trying to keep his voice down.

"Don't you trust the police to do their jobs?" Grace asked him loudly, clearly trying to put him in a bad spot. I couldn't even blame her. After all, she was only doing it out of loyalty to her husband and me.

"Of course I do. I trust them completely," he said, matching if not exceeding her volume. I had to give it to Max. When he wanted it to, his voice could cut through the loudest crowd. In fact, when we'd been married, we'd been at a pop-up Renaissance fair near Charlotte, and I'd heard his distinct laughter in the midst of a horde of crying babies, amplified lute music, and a host of screaming drunks yelling "Huzza" at the tops of their lungs. "Come on, Grace, cut me some slack. If Suzanne can forgive me, why can't you?" he asked as he lowered his voice to a more conversational level.

"I suppose she's just a better person than I am," Grace said with a wicked smile.

"Okay, let's all just take a deep breath and calm down," I said, trying to play the role of mediator. "Max, we are *already* looking into this, so don't think we're doing it just for you, but you could certainly help us with some background." I'd come up with the idea while he and Grace had been engaging in verbal warfare, but the more I considered it, the more I liked it. After all, we had no connections inside this theatrical world Max inhabited, so it would be hard to break through without getting some help from the inside.

"I'd be happy to do that," Max said, "but the person you should really talk to is Hillary Teal."

"She makes costumes for your productions, doesn't she?" I asked.

"Yes, but Hillary does much more than that. If there's something going on behind the scenes, Hillary knows about it. She's your girl."

Calling Hillary a girl was an amazing abuse of the English language. Hillary hadn't been a girl since Eisenhower had been president, but I knew what Max meant. She might have been old chronologically, but she was certainly a girl when it came to her outlook on life. The woman always seemed as though the world around her had been built solely for her own amusement.

"Give her a call and have her meet us at my place in ten minutes," I told him.

"Seriously? You expect her to just show up at your beck and call?" Max asked.

Before Grace could interject, I said, "No, I expect her to show up at *yours*. Max, if you can't get her to cooperate with us, I don't know how you expect us to help you."

"I'll call her," he said, though he made no move to do as he'd just promised.

"Sounds good. We'll wait," I said serenely.

"You want me to call her this instant?"

I just smiled, and though there wasn't much affection in mine, Grace's grin was positively chilling.

"Fine," Max agreed reluctantly.

It took him less than a minute to convince Hillary to do as we'd asked. After he hung up, he turned to me and asked, "Is there anything else I can do?"

It wasn't like he'd done all that much, but I didn't feel as though it was all that polite to point it out to him. "Tell us about Hal Embry."

"Okay, but let's do it outside," he said as he looked around. I noticed that Officer Handler had been watching us, so I followed Max out of the auditorium, tugging Grace along to go with me.

"What's up with Rick?" Grace asked me softly once we were past him.

"I'm not sure, but I think he might be unhappy that he was passed over for the second-in-command post," I told her.

"Stephen thought about it, but in the end, he decided that Darby had more potential."

"Ouch. I bet that left a mark," I said.

"He didn't actually *tell* him that," Grace said. "Give Stephen a little more credit than that."

"I do," I said. "I was just teasing you."

We were all outside, and though we were in the full bloom of spring, there was still quite a bite in the air. We'd been known to get freak snowfalls in April and even May in our neck of the woods, though they were pretty rare. Still, it wasn't out of the question. We might have been living in the South, but we were still perched in the foothills of the Blue Ridge Mountains.

I pulled my jacket a bit closer and rubbed my hands together before sticking them into my pockets. Grace did the same as Max said, "Man, it's chilly out here. Can we walk over to the donut shop and get out of the cold?"

"There aren't any donuts left, Max," I told him.

"Fine, but you can still make us a pot of hot coffee, can't you?"

"I could, but I'm not going to," I said. "The second folks in town see the lights on in Donut Hearts, we'll have people interrupting us the rest of the night."

"That's a fair point," Max said. "I'm going to make this brief though."

"Fine. You were about to tell us about Hal Embry," I reminded him.

Max frowned for a second. "Hal considered himself a method actor. Nobody could talk to him half an hour before a performance, and when they did, they would get the character he was playing, not the man. Hal would do anything to immerse himself in a role, and I mean anything."

"Tell us about the part he was set to play tonight," I said.

"Johnny Love is a real reprobate. He's a cad in the classic sense of the word, cheating and stealing and lying his way through high school until there's not a soul around who doesn't want to see him dead."

"Wow, was Hal anything like that in real life?" Grace asked him.

"A month ago, I would have said no way, but the second he read the script, he changed. I'd seen it before in other productions, but he was taking it too far this time. He's been dating Karen Lexington since both of their spouses died, and everyone thought they'd get married someday. But since getting this role, Hal has been running his lines with every leading lady in the production, and I don't mean just acting. Last night, Karen finally had enough, and she stormed on stage and threatened Hal with castration. It was pretty intense."

"Is she in the play as well?" I asked.

"Yes, she's got a bit part midway through the production, ironically playing one of the few girls in school that Johnny *doesn't* want to sleep with."

"Who are his love interests in the play?" I asked.

"The main three are Jenny, Amy, and Erica," he said.

"What are their last names?" I asked. I knew a few Jennys, an Amy, and I had a cousin named Erica. Surely *she* wasn't in this play. She was much too young to play a student at Max's particular high school.

"Those are their character names," Max said. "The women themselves are Celia Laslow from Maple Hollow, Geraldine Morgan from Union Square, and Vivian Crowe from here in town."

"I didn't realize you cast your parts from all over the area," Grace said.

"There aren't enough seniors in April Springs to play all of the roles," Max explained. "Besides, when I bring in actors from all over the area, it's more likely we'll be able to sell out our performances."

"Who knew you were that savvy," I said.

"As the production's producer, it's one of my jobs to fill those seats," he said. "We need to clear a healthy profit on our shows in order to continue having them." After a moment, he said, "I don't know how we're going to get through this one."

"I wouldn't worry about that if I were you," I said.

"What do you mean?"

"When you finally do have your opening night, folks from all around are going to flock to see your killer play." It was a poor choice of words, and I knew it the second they left my mouth. "You know what I mean," I added.

"Do you honestly think that's true?" Max asked hopefully.

"If what's happened at the donut shop in the past is any indication, I can just about guarantee it," I said.

"Who was Hal's understudy?" Grace asked. "After all, if he can't go on, which obviously he can't, who gets the role now?"

"You honestly don't think someone would commit murder for a role in a local theater production, do you, Grace?" Max asked.

"Suzanne and I have seen people killed for less reason than that," she said.

"It's true enough," I agreed.

"Well, I think you're both off base this time. Zane Whitlow is going to be taking over for Hal now, but Zane wouldn't hurt a fly. He can handle the role. In fact, I was afraid that he was going to have to take over tonight, but Hal showed up at the last second, so Zane gave Hal his jacket and stepped aside. He's a real trouper."

"We'll talk to Zane, anyway," I said. I knew Zane, and I could understand Max's reservations. Zane Whitlow was a quiet older man who had barely said ten words to me in all the time I'd known him. How could a man that quiet and reserved act on stage in front of the entire town, and more folks than that to boot? "I can't imagine Zane acting on stage."

"Wait until you see him. He really comes alive," Max said with animation. "The truth is that I almost cast him in the lead this time, but Hal threatened to walk out of the production if I did, and I needed him."

"Was he really that big a draw?" I asked.

Max looked around before he said softly, "No, but he financed this show out of his own pocket, so I couldn't exactly cut him out of it and expect him to still be our angel, could I?" He turned to Grace and explained, "An angel is someone who..."

She cut him off before he could continue mansplaining the concept to her. "Who backs plays financially and gets a cut of the profits if and when the show breaks even."

Max looked at my best friend with new respect. "That's true enough in most cases, but I doubt Hal ever expected to recoup his investment, let alone make a profit. It was just his way of being sure that he got the juiciest roles to play." Max looked thoughtful for a moment before he added, "I didn't even consider that. Now I need to find a new angel too."

"Well, don't look at us. Suzanne's as poor as a church mouse, and I wouldn't dump free water on you if you were on fire." Grace added with a fake smile, "With all due respect. No offense intended."

"None taken," Max said, dismissing her with a wave of his hand.

I was about to ask my ex another question when the poor woman who had discovered that Hal had been murdered came rushing toward us. "Max! Oh, Max! What a tragedy!"

"It's going to be okay, Celia," he said as he fought off her enthusiastic embrace. I wasn't sure how Emily, Max's latest wife, would feel about that, but I realized at that moment that I hadn't seen her at her husband's big debut.

"Where is your *wife*, Max?" I asked, trying to learn the answer as well as dissuade Celia from her embrace.

"She stayed home. She was feeling a bit under the weather tonight," Max said.

"The poor dear. She doesn't have the stamina we women of a certain age have," Celia said smugly.

"Celia, would it be possible for Grace and I to have a second of your time?" I asked her before she salivated all over my ex-husband. I had to admit that it was fun watching him squirm, but I really did want to talk to her about Hal.

"I couldn't possibly," she said, shedding a few more crocodile tears. "I must go home. Max, be a dear and drive me to Maple Hollow."

"I can't," Max said flatly. I had to give him credit for that. He'd never make it out of April Springs alive once he was alone in the car with that woman.

"We'll be more than happy to drive you," I volunteered. Grace looked at me askance, so I added, "We'll just have to postpone our other appointments." I was bluffing, but Celia didn't know it, and neither did Grace.

Once the actress realized that Max wasn't going to take her anywhere, let alone home, she pulled herself from him as she said, "Silly me. I just remembered that I drove myself here tonight, so of course I need to drive back."

"That sounds good. We'll be in touch tomorrow," I told her as she started away.

"Why on earth would you want to do that?" Celia asked me coolly.

"We'd love to get your take on what happened to Hal," Grace said in a conspiratorial whisper.

Celia looked reluctant, and then my ex spoke up. "Talk to them, Celia. Do it for me," Max cajoled her gently.

"For you? Of course. Here's my card," Celia said as she handed me a business card. I studied it for a second, but there was no business listed on it. It simply had her name, phone number, and address embossed on it. It was an actual calling card! I hadn't seen one of those since I'd been a kid.

After she was gone, Max said, "Thanks for saving me."

I ignored his gratitude. "Is Emily all right?"

"She's fine. At least she will be. I'll tell her you were asking about her."

"Do that," I said. I was about to ask him something else when Officer Handler came outside and started toward us.

"Mr. Thornburg, if I may have another word," he called out.

"Sorry, but it appears that he wants you, not us," I said as I grabbed Grace's arm and headed for my Jeep.

There was nothing Max could do about it, and as we got into my vehicle and drove back to my house, I could see Max being questioned again by our local police.

I felt a little bad about him being cornered like that, but there was nothing I could do about it.

After all, Grace and I had other things on our plate at the moment.

Chapter 3

"WE'RE CUTTING IT KIND of close having Hillary meet us at the cottage when Darby's coming by later, aren't we?" Grace asked me as we passed her house.

"You know me. I live for danger," I told her with a slight smile.

"I don't know if I'd say that," she answered.

"Grace, we have to push things while we can. I'm afraid Darby's going to come to his senses any second and realize that he shouldn't give us any standing in this case, official or otherwise."

"I thought at the time you were a little nuts asking him," Grace admitted as I pulled into my driveway. I was happy to see a Cadillac older than I was parked there.

"Hillary's already here," I said as I got out of the Jeep.

The petite older woman was sitting patiently on the front porch, even though there was a steady chill in the air. At least she was bundled in her coat, a garment that seemed to swallow her entire body up in its folds.

"I'm sorry you had to wait outside," I said as I grabbed my keys and opened the front door.

Hillary's hair was the oddest shade of brunette I'd ever seen, and I was certain that it had come from a bottle and not from nature. "I don't mind the cool fresh air," she said flatly as she stared out into the darkness. "I want to enjoy it while I still can." I'd always thought of her as a cheerful woman, but the murder had clearly affected her, because her normal spark was gone.

"I can't blame you for that," I said, trying to make my voice a bit lighter in the hopes of cheering her up. "I, on the other hand, like a good warm fire and a mug of tea, cocoa, or coffee on a night like this."

"Cocoa? I haven't had that in years," she said as she shook her head. "Don't go to any extra trouble for me, but if you're having some, I'd love a cup myself."

I turned to Grace. "How about you?"

"Make it three," she said with a nod as we all stepped inside the cottage.

I got busy in the kitchen, and the other women joined me. "It was tragic what happened tonight, wasn't it?" I asked Hillary.

"Yes, but not all that unpredictable," the costumer said with a sudden frown.

"Are you saying that you weren't surprised that Hal was murdered right there on stage tonight?" I asked her.

"Of course I was," Hillary said with a hint of despair in her voice. "It's just that he's been toying with some of the other cast members' affections. I warned him that he was taking his acting method too far, but he wouldn't listen to me."

"Was it really all acting, or was Hal just a cad at heart, and the role gave him the chance to exercise his true inner self?" Grace asked.

It was an odd way to put the question, and it took me a second to realize that Grace was using Hillary's own speech patterns to question her. Whether she was doing it consciously or not I couldn't say.

"He could be quite charming when he put his mind to it," Hillary said softly.

I had a hunch and decided to pursue it. "Did he try to charm *you*, by any chance?"

Hillary bit her lower lip for a moment, and then she shrugged. "He tried, but he was entirely unsuccessful," she answered. "It's a pity you couldn't say the same thing about his other attempts."

"How did his girlfriend deal with his behavior?" I asked.

"As of yesterday, Karen Lexington was no longer his girlfriend, if that gives you any indication," Hillary said as I handed her a mug of hot chocolate. She looked at the mug and then frowned for a second. "No marshmallows?"

"I have baby ones," I said as I got out the bag. After I dropped three into hers, I did the same to mine and Grace's before I handed hers over.

"That brings back memories," Hillary said after she took a sip. "It's actually quite good," she added as she continued staring into her mug. "They've made some real improvements in hot chocolate mixes since the last time I tasted any."

"It's a special blend we use at Donut Hearts," I told her. "Would you like some to take with you?"

"If it's not too much trouble," she answered.

As I put some of our mix into a clean used jam jar, I said, "You could add water to the mix if you'd like, but I much prefer warmed milk."

"As do I," she said.

"Were you at the theatre when Karen broke up with Hal?" I asked her.

"So, I wasn't the first person to mention the breakup to you," Hillary said.

"We heard someone say something about it," I admitted. "How bad was it?"

"Bad enough that I was embarrassed to witness it," Hillary admitted. "Unfortunately, not everyone there agreed. The smiles on Celia's, Geraldine's, and Vivian's faces were vulgar, to say the least." Hillary actually shuddered at the memory of it.

"Was he actually trying to ... woo all three of them?" I asked her.

"Woo. What a wonderful word from a different time. I wouldn't say what Hal was doing was quite as old-fashioned and romantic as that. The truth of the matter is that he was trying to do quite a bit more than woo them, if you'll excuse my crassness."

"And did he succeed?" Grace asked her.

"In at least one case, and possibly all three," Hillary said as she shook her head.

"Do you think one of them might have done it?" I asked her gently.

She shrugged. "Were they unhappy with him? Certainly. But murder? I have no idea."

"Well, pardon my bluntness," I said, "but *someone* killed Hal Embry. I certainly don't think it was suicide." Then I wondered if that might be a possibility after all. Stabbing yourself in the chest with a sharp knife wasn't the way most people ended their own lives, but I had to wonder if the angle of the blade even made that a possibility. I'd have to ask Darby when I got the chance.

"I know. I'm still having a difficult time accepting that it all really happened. I honestly think I'm still in shock," Hillary said as she took another long drink from her hot chocolate.

"What about Zane Whitlow?" I asked her. "Could you see him doing it?"

"To get a role? That's not possible. Besides, Zane is a gentle man with a good heart. I couldn't believe it when Max cast him as the understudy to Hal Embry. The two men couldn't have been any more different."

"So, Zane wasn't a womanizer?" Grace asked her.

"Not from anything I've heard," Hillary said adamantly. "He is an excellent actor, though. If there's a silver lining to this, which I'm sure there isn't, it's that the world will learn that Zane is an amazing man."

"It sounds as though you might like him a bit yourself," I suggested.

Her face reddened a bit, which surprised me. Hillary didn't seem the type to me to get flustered about anything. "Nonsense. He doesn't even know I'm alive."

"I'm guessing you're wrong there," I said.

She looked at me a bit hopefully. "Really? Why do you say that?"

"You fitted him for his costume, didn't you?" I asked.

"Yes, of course. That's my job."

"So, he at least knows you are alive," I answered.

"Not in *that* way, though," she corrected me.

After Hillary finished her hot chocolate, I asked, "Would you like a refill? There's plenty where that came from."

"No, I really mustn't. Mother will worry about me if I stay out too late."

I'd completely forgotten that Hillary's mother was still alive. From what I'd heard, it had been years since she'd left the house they shared. "How is she?"

"Over ninety and as full of herself as she ever was," she said a bit ruefully. "If I don't make it home soon, she'll have the police out searching for me."

Hillary stood and handed me her empty mug. "Thank you for the cocoa, and the extra batch as well," she said as she held up the jar. "I'm sorry I couldn't be of much help."

"I'm happy to do it," I said. "Before you go, I'd just like to ask you one more question," I said.

As she got into her coat, she said, "The truth of the matter is that I really didn't see much of anything tonight, ladies. I was busy doing last-minute alterations on Vivian's dress. She's put on a few pounds since her first fitting, though she denies it vehemently."

"Did you happen to see anyone near Hal before the curtain went up?" I asked her.

"I don't believe that I saw anything out of the ordinary."

Was it just me, or had she hesitated before she'd said that last bit? I wasn't sure, but one look at Grace told me that she'd caught it as well.

"You're among friends here, Hillary," I told her. "Anything you tell us will be strictly confidential. We're just trying to help."

"I know all about the two of you," she said with a sigh. "You're the famous amateur sleuths of April Springs. I'm sorry I couldn't be more help, but I'm certain the two of you will unmask the killer and save the day in the end." She said the last bit as though it was an effort for her to even speak. The murder must have taken more out of her than she was even showing us.

Hillary seemed distracted as we walked her out to her car. The beast started right up, and she drove away into the night without a single glance back in our direction.

"Was it just me, or was Hillary hiding something from us right before she left?" I asked Grace once she was gone.

"It wasn't just you," she said. "Wow, that was close. Here comes Acting Chief Jones, right on time."

"That's kind of a clunky title, isn't it?" I asked as the temporary top cop for April Springs pulled into the spot Hillary had just vacated.

"I don't care. I'm not going to call him Chief Jones, not with Stephen still in charge around here," Grace said resolutely.

"I don't think there's a chance in the world that Darby Jones even wants your husband's job," I told her.

"I should hope not," Grace said as he got out and joined us.

"Was that Hillary Teal I just saw leaving?" Darby asked.

"She wanted some hot chocolate mix," I told him. It was the truth, though just part of it. I knew the acting chief had given us his blessing to snoop around a bit, but I also realized that the permission was tenuous at best.

"What did she have to say about tonight?" he asked, not accepting my explanation at all.

"She told us she didn't see a thing," I told him a bit snappily, "and for the record, you can call her and ask her yourself. She left here with a belly full of cocoa and a jam jar full of mix, and that's all that happened."

"I don't doubt that for one second," Darby said. "Come on, I thought we were on the same side here, ladies."

"We are," I said, taking a more gentle tone with him. "She did tell us that Hal was catting around on the side with the three main actresses."

"And we heard that Karen, his girlfriend, broke up with him last night because of it," Grace added.

I hadn't been at all certain I was going to share that particular fact just yet, but we were cooperating with the acting police chief, so it made sense to tell him everything we'd heard. The truth was that we weren't investigating for the credit; all we wanted was for someone *not* to get away with murder.

"Yeah, somebody mentioned that," he said. "Did you find out anything else?"

I shook my head. "No, but in our defense, we just got started. How about you? Any luck at the crime scene?"

"There were no prints on the blade," he admitted. "It was a long shot, but I was hoping the killer got sloppy."

"I thought they'd use a prop knife for that scene," I said.

"They had one, but nobody can find it. The one that was used to kill Hal was close enough to the prop to be mistaken for it."

"There's no chance this was just some horrible kind of accident, is there?" I asked. "Can you imagine someone thinking they had the prop knife and using the real one instead?" The mere thought gave me chills.

"Not unless it was suicide," Darby said.

That brought up the question I was holding for him. "Is there any chance that it could have *been* suicide?" I asked him.

"The doc said no when I asked her about it. The angle of the blade was all wrong, but it was a good thought."

"How was the knife *supposed* to be attached?" Grace asked him.

"From what I gather, Embry was supposed to place the knife himself," he replied.

"Just out of curiosity, but who was in charge of the prop table?" I asked.

"That would be your ex-husband," Darby said with a frown.

Chapter 4

"I CAN'T IMAGINE MAX doing anything wrong," I blurted out.

"Take it easy, Suzanne. Nobody's accusing him of anything."

"Did anyone else have access to that table?" Grace asked.

"Every member of the cast and crew," Darby admitted a bit miserably. "But there's no way Hal would have mistaken a real knife for the prop one, according to Max. It wasn't suicide, and it wasn't an accident. It was murder, plain and simple. How the killer managed to do it without anyone seeing it happen is beyond me."

"Darby, you interviewed everyone who was backstage," I said. "Did *anyone* see anything out of the ordinary?"

"Not that they were willing to share with me," the acting chief admitted.

"Do you think someone's holding out on you?" I asked, killing the added "too" at the last second. I wasn't sure I was ready to throw Hillary to the wolves just yet, at least not until Grace and I had a chance to push her a little harder the next day.

"It wouldn't surprise me a bit," Darby said. "I should have the official results of the autopsy tomorrow, but I can't imagine that the cause of death *wasn't* a single stab wound through the chest straight into the heart. The means and the opportunity are both shared by a dozen folks. If we're going to figure this out, it's got to be about the motive."

It touched me that he'd said "we." "And from the look of things, motive is the one thing we have plenty of for our list of suspects," I said.

"Do you happen to have an *actual* list?" he asked me curiously. "Because from what I've seen, it could have been *any* of the twelve folks I've been focused on tonight."

"Is Max among that number?" I asked him, trying to keep the emotion out of my voice.

"Suzanne, don't get riled up. We both know that he has to be."

As Darby started to explain further, I interrupted him. Why was I suddenly being *overprotective* of my ex-husband? Sometimes even *I* didn't understand the things I said and did. "I'm not blaming you. I understand why you have to consider him. I just don't see him as viable here."

"Neither do I, but until I have a way of narrowing things down a bit, he has to stay right where he is," Darby said.

"I can live with that," I said, "but I think the first folks we should focus on are Karen Lexington, Celia Laslow, Geraldine Morgan, Vivian Crowe, and Zane Whitlow."

"Zane? Really?" the acting chief asked. "The man's as meek and mild as they come."

"Maybe so, but he was Hal Embry's understudy, which makes him next in line for the part, so he can't be ruled out," I said. "Do you agree, Grace?" She nodded, but I could tell that something was bothering her. "Is there anyone *else* you can think of?"

"I'd have to add Hillary Teal to the list," she said.

So, the earlier omission had bothered her even more than it had me.

"Why is that?" Darby asked her.

"She has...had a pretty strong opinion about the way Hal was acting with the other cast members. It might be nothing, but then again, he might have offended her moral code somehow. Who knows? I just think we need to keep her on the list as a suspect for now."

"Agreed," I said. "I'm afraid that's all we have for tonight, Officer...Chief...I don't know what to call you."

"Officer Jones in public, Darby in private are both fine with me," he said. He then looked at Grace. "I wish this was in your husband's lap and not mine, and I'll be happier to see him back in April Springs than you will be."

It went a long way to easing Grace's feelings about the man as I saw the glacier under the surface start to thaw. "I sincerely doubt that," she answered with a grin. "Don't sweat it. You'll be okay, Darby."

"With your help, I hope so," he said as his radio squawked. He answered, and after a moment, he turned back to us. "I've got to go, ladies. Stay in touch, okay?"

"Was that about the case?" I asked him as he got into his squad car.

"No, it's about a stolen bicycle that I'm not a hundred percent sure was stolen and not sold," he said. "The joys of small-town living."

"I wouldn't trade it for the world, though," I said.

"Well, maybe except for the murders," Grace added.

"Yeah, there's always that," I said.

After Darby was gone, Grace said, "Suzanne, suddenly I don't feel like going home. Would you like some company tonight?" I stifled a yawn, and before I could answer, she added quickly, "Strike that. Tomorrow's a workday for both of us."

"I appreciate that. Will you be able to help me after I close the donut shop tomorrow?" I asked her.

"Oh, yes. I've got some paperwork waiting for me on my desk that is going to prove to be particularly difficult, at least until it's too late for me to do anything else for the rest of the day, other than help you, that is. At least that's going to be my story if anyone asks," she answered with a grin.

"Thanks. That means a lot to me." I glanced at the clock. "You know, it's really not that late. We could watch a movie or something if you'd like."

"Go to bed. That's an order, young lady. I'll be fine on my own."

"I know you will. You're always more than fine, and you know it. In fact, I think you're spectacular."

"Right back at you," Grace said as she walked up the road to her house.

I felt bad about not insisting that she stay later and hang around, but tomorrow would come too soon as things stood, and if I was going to be able to make donuts and solve a murder, I was going to need my sleep.

I wished that I could call Jake, bring him up to speed, and even say good night to him, but unfortunately, that wasn't going to be an option. I'd just have to bide my time until he got back into cell phone range.

As I nodded off to sleep, I kept seeing Hal Embry slumped over in that seat, wearing his tux, that silly prom king crown perched on his head, and a knife plunged deep into his chest.

Unfortunately for him, the king was dead, and it was up to Grace and me to figure out who had done it.

"Good morning, sunshine," I told Emma the next morning as she came back into the kitchen of Donut Hearts. It was a little after four a.m., early for most folks, but I'd already been at the shop for an hour.

"Morning," she said, stifling a yawn. "Sorry about that. I was up late working on plans for the restaurant. Sometimes I wish Mom and I hadn't inherited that money. I know we'll be happy making Barton's dreams come true, but wow, has it been a ton of work."

"We both know that it wasn't a purely altruistic move on your part," I told her with a smile. "I can't imagine *any* restaurant that Barton runs not being wildly successful. Just remember me fondly when you're both rich and famous," I told her.

"As if," she answered. "I don't care one speck about fame." After a moment's thought, she added with a slight smile, "I wouldn't mind the money, though."

"Come on. You'll be a hot property owning the coolest place in four counties," I told her.

"Well, this hot property just wants to bury her arms in warm, sudsy water and get started on those dishes."

It was odd that Emma hadn't said anything about Hal Embry's murder at the theater the night before. I had braced myself for a barrage of questions, originating with her father no doubt, so that was a happy surprise. One thing was certain: if she didn't bring it up, I certainly wasn't going to.

As I finished up the cake donuts for the day, I asked her, "What's the latest snag you're running into with the restaurant?"

"It appears we are going to have to change the name," Emma said. "The Bistro isn't distinctive enough, and Barton wants something more cosmopolitan than even that. He suggested the letter B, but Mom and I both vetoed it."

"B as in Barton, or B as in Bistro?" I asked.

"B as in both, I suspect," she said as she dove into the dishes. "Mom thinks people will think it's a honey-based restaurant."

"I can see that happening around here," I said with a laugh. "Just think of the possibilities. You could have yellow and black tiles on the floor, yellow and black tablecloths, and a pot of honey on every table. The local beekeepers would love you."

"Maybe so, but that's not exactly our target audience," Emma answered.

"What are *your* thoughts?"

"I started with BES, but that's no good," she said. "Then Mom suggested SharBarEm."

"It doesn't exactly roll off the tongue, does it?"

"Not so much," she admitted. "We considered Barton's, Gleason's, and Blake's, but we don't want to discount the other two owners."

"What street is it on?" I asked her.

"Twenty-first," she said. "Why?"

"How about Twenty-First Southern?" I asked. "It has the added benefit of including the street name in it as well as the current century. Barton puts his own unique spin on things, so it sounds modern and traditional at the same time."

"That might just work," she said. "Do you mind if we steal it if my partners are okay with it?"

"It's yours. I just have one condition."

"What is it? Do you want your own table, reserved just for you? If this works, you can name your own price."

"I don't want anything that grand," I said. "I would like a table for four on opening night. I know you're going to be jammed with reservations, and we'll pay for our own food, but I'd love to celebrate your grand opening with you."

"It's a deal. We'll pick up the tab, though. It's the least we can do."

"Don't be giving away food," I told her. "You need to make a profit, remember?"

"I'm sorry, but that's nonnegotiable. If you come, there won't be a bill. Come on, I know you let the DeAngelis clan at Napoli's comp your meals sometimes in Union Square."

"That's different," I protested.

"Why? Do you love them more than you do me?" She asked the question facetiously, batting her eyes at me like some kind of innocent lamb.

I had to laugh. "Okay, you win. But just for opening night."

"We'll see," Emma said with a chuckle that matched my own. As she continued to wash dirty pots and pans, she added, "I can't believe what happened at the theater last night. It was all Dad could talk about."

I had a hunch that it had been too good to last. "Yes, it was terrible." I might have been more involved in the case than she realized, so if I downplayed it, maybe I'd still get away relatively unscathed.

"You were there, weren't you?"

"Grace and I went together," I admitted. "We were shocked by what happened just as much as everyone else was."

"I bet," Emma said as she turned back to her dishes.

I knew word would get around quickly enough that Grace and I were digging into the murder, but at the moment, it seemed like we were still under everyone else's radar, which was exactly where I wanted to be.

"Twenty-First Southern," Emma repeated a few times. "I really like that."

"Hey, it's all part of the service here at Donut Hearts. We provide names to anyone in need: businesses, friends, and strangers alike."

"I don't remember seeing that on the menu, but I'm glad it's offered here," Emma said.

"Suzanne? Is that you?" a man about my age asked as he studied the cases of donuts behind me. "It's me."

"Hello, me," I said, not having a clue as to who he might be. We'd been open barely an hour, but the customers had been coming in at a steady pace.

"You don't recognize me, do you?" he asked with a hint of offense in his voice.

I studied him for a moment. Thinning hair, bulging belly, jowls that needed a shave, and shoes that could use a polish. His jeans were a bit worn, and his shirt collar was frayed. No, I had no idea who he was.

"I'm sorry, but I wait on a great many people in the course of a day."

"I'm not a *customer*," he said. "It's me. Grady."

I'd only known one Grady in my life, a boy I'd had a crush on in the ninth grade. He'd been captain of the football team and a member of the Honor Society to boot, and I hadn't been the only girl who'd mooned over him.

"Grady *Hasburger*?" I asked incredulously.

"One and the same," he said proudly.

"What...how have you been?" I'd nearly asked him what had happened to him, but that was evident enough. He'd gotten older, though maybe a little less gracefully than some of the rest of us had.

"I've been great," he said. He looked me up and down as though he was preparing to bid on me when he said, "Wow, you turned out nice."

"Thank you," I said, not sure how to take his comment.

"Personally, I *like* a gal with some meat on her bones. More to grab hold of, if you know what I mean," he added with a conspiratorial little whisper. "It's your lucky day, Suzanne. I'm free since my divorce. What say you and me go out on the town tonight?"

"I'm not sure my husband would appreciate that," I said, doing my best not to show my displeasure at the very suggestion.

He actually winked at me. "That's fine by me. I won't tell him if you won't."

"Trust me, he'd find out. He's a state police inspector," I replied, not mentioning that Jake was now retired. "Can I get you something, Grady?"

He honestly seemed surprised that I hadn't jumped all over his invitation. "Yeah, give me a couple of dozen donuts."

It took all I had not to ask him if he was going to eat them at the shop or if he wanted them to go. As I boxed them up, he asked, "Whatever happened to Grace Gauge? Is she still in town?"

"She is," I said as his eyes lit up. "She's married to the chief of police."

He frowned at that news. "Man, everybody's hitched just when I'm free and back on the prowl."

I didn't ask him what he was doing back in April Springs, mainly because I didn't care.

When he realized that I wasn't going to pose the question, he supplied the answer himself. "I came into some money, so I thought I'd look up some of the old gang."

"Well, good luck with that," I said. "That'll be nineteen eighty-five for the donuts."

He looked genuinely surprised that I'd had the audacity to ask him to pay. "Even for an old friend like me?"

I wanted to tell him that because of his crack about my weight, I almost charged him double, but I just put on my most plastic smile. "Sorry. I can't play favorites."

"I get it," he said as he grudgingly pulled out a ten, eight ones, and enough change to make up the difference. If he'd come into money, it must have been from robbing his childhood piggy bank.

As Grady grabbed the donuts and headed for the front door, I called out, "You have yourself a nice day."

"Yeah. Sure."

For some reason, I kind of doubted he'd be a repeat customer while he was back in town, but I had a feeling that I'd be fine without his business.

Wow, was I happy I hadn't taken that particular road way back when.

I couldn't wait to tell Grace. As a matter of fact, I called her the second there was a lull in the crowd of customers. "You'll never believe who came by the donut shop a few minutes ago."

"Darby? Did he have anything new on the case?" she asked.

"No, this is more like a blast from our past. Grady Hasburger stopped in."

"Grady? Seriously? We both had such crushes on him way back then."

"Well, you can have him if you want him; he's newly divorced. He wanted to go out with me, but when he found I was married, he asked me about you."

"I hope you told him that I was married too," she said. "Just out of curiosity, how has he held up since high school?"

After I described him to her in graphic detail, I added his comment about me having meat on my bones. "It took all I had not to smack him with a donut."

"I wish you had," she said. "What a loser."

I was about to comment when I saw Karen Lexington approaching the shop. "Listen, I've got to go. I'll see you in a bit."

"Is someone there? Is it Darby? Suzanne, talk to me," Grace pled.

"Bye," I said, hating to cut her off, but I wanted to be able to give Karen my complete focus.

I wasn't sure why she was at Donut Hearts, but I needed to talk to her about Hal Embry and if by any chance she'd had something to do with that knife in his chest.

Chapter 5

"HELLO, SUZANNE," KAREN said as she walked into the shop, dressed all in black. I wasn't completely sure if she was in mourning or if it was just some kind of fashion statement. Karen wasn't one of my customers at Donut Hearts ordinarily, so I couldn't really say.

"Hi, Karen. I'm so sorry about Hal," I told her sympathetically. "It must have been a real blow losing him like that."

"It was tragic. I don't know if you've heard, but we were in the middle of a minor little squabble when it happened," she said softly. "I'm afraid that things got a little bit out of hand a few nights ago. He was letting this role go to his head, and I tried to reason with him, to no avail, I'm sorry to say. I thought he'd come around after I chastised him about his behavior, but we'll never know now, will we?" Quite a bit louder, she added for the crowd, "I can't believe someone robbed me of the one true love of my life."

I thought she was laying it on a little thick, but then again, maybe she didn't want anyone to think that *she* might have been the one who had killed him. Goodness knows she certainly had reasons enough of her own to make the suspect list. "I heard you two had more than just a squabble," I pointed out just as loudly myself.

Karen looked at me askance as though she was shocked that I'd had the audacity to call her on what I'd heard. It was clear the woman was playing to the crowd in Donut Hearts, pretending to be the grief-stricken lover instead of actually being one. No wonder she hadn't qualified for a role as one of the three main girls after the prom king. If this was her acting at its best, she needed some work. "You know what it's like. People in the theater tend to exaggerate a bit," she said.

"That's probably what it was," I said, not believing it for a second but not wanting to drive her off until I had a chance to speak with her a little bit further. Lowering my voice back to a conversational level, I asked, "Karen, since you were the one person in town closest to Hal, who do you think did it?"

"It had to be one of the three tarts," she said. "I'm sure of it."

"Pardon me?" I asked.

"Oh, that's what we call them in our little troupe, that or the three merry widows. Technically just Celia and Geraldine are true widows, but Vivian is a black widow if ever there were one."

"They can't *all* have done it," I said. "Surely you have a favorite."

Karen shook her head. "If I were to lay money on it, I'd bet on Celia, but you didn't hear that from me."

"Understood. When was the last time you spoke to Hal?" I wanted to pin her down so I had a chance to disprove or prove her claim later.

"It pains me to say that it was during our little tiff," Karen replied, and then she dabbed at her dry cheek with a white lace handkerchief.

I tried my best to look surprised. "Are you saying that you didn't talk to him at all yesterday?"

She shrugged. "There was nothing of substance said, at any rate. I may have told him to break a leg, but I shared that sentiment with the entire cast."

"I mean something a little more...intimate," I said softly.

"No, nothing," she said emphatically.

"Did you happen to see anyone speaking to him *before* the dress rehearsal last night?" I asked her.

"Not personally, but I heard that he and Zane had some strong words before he stormed off."

"I'm sorry. Which one stormed off where?" I asked.

"Evidently Zane said something to Hal, who just laughed at him, Zane, and then he, Zane, walked off stage with fire in his, Zane's, eyes while he, Hal, continued to chuckle long after he, Zane, was gone. Is that clear enough for you?"

She was so condescending it was all I could do not to reach across the counter and swat her with the towel in my hand.

"I understand," I said. "Do you have any idea what they were discussing?"

"Not a clue," Karen said. "I was in the wardrobe room, working on my costume. I've had an ongoing argument with Hillary, the woman in charge of our costumes, that my bodice should be a bit tighter, but she refused to alter it any more. I don't have all that many lines, so I have to make do with my physical characteristics and mannerisms instead," she answered. "It's what acting is all about, being noticed."

I wasn't at all sure that was true, but then again, it wouldn't do me any good arguing with her about it. "Did Hillary happen to say anything to Hal before the performance?"

"As I said, I have no idea. I did hear that she tried to speak with Zane though, but he brushed her off. I believe she's smitten with the man. Are you kidding me? Who develops a crush on an *understudy?*" She made the last word sound as though it was some kind of slur, and to her, there was no doubt in my mind that it was. "It's like falling for the drummer of a rock-and-roll band."

I knew of some pretty nice-looking drummers, but again, I decided to keep my mouth shut about it. "Will the play go on, do you think?" I asked her, more out of curiosity than anything else. After all, if Zane had killed Hal to get the role, it would be all for naught if the show didn't take place.

"You'd have to ask your husband about that," she said.

"Why would Jake know anything about that?" I asked her.

"Not that one. The first one. Maxwell," she said.

Not even Max's mother had called him Maxwell. "I'll do that."

Karen looked around the shop, waved to one or two of my customers, and then she started for the door. Evidently she'd done what she'd come to do, which was to proclaim her innocence in front of as many people as she could find.

"Don't you want a donut while you're here?"

"No, I just had a full breakfast at the Boxcar Grill," she said. "I thought I might get something for later, but I've changed my mind."

So my original suspicion was true. This *wasn't* her first show of the morning. Karen had already performed at the Boxcar, and I had to wonder where she was headed next. No doubt she was hoping to sway the court of public opinion in her favor, but I doubted it would do her much good.

If she'd killed her estranged boyfriend, what the rest of April Springs thought didn't really matter. She had an audience of one she had to convince, and at the moment, that was Acting Police Chief Darby Jones.

Still, her commentary gave me food for thought. Had Hal and Zane really argued just before the star of the show had been murdered? Was Vivian a black widow, killing a man who might have rejected her? Or had one of the other actresses done it? I had to keep all of the cast and crewmembers in the mix as well, including Max and Hillary.

I was just about to turn my back on the front when something outside caught the corner of my eye. It was Officer Handler, otherwise known as Rick in more usual circumstances, and he appeared to be having a rather intimate conversation with Karen Lexington in front of my shop. They were standing much too close to each other to be strangers, and I had to wonder what it was all about when the police officer surprised me by hugging her before heading into the donut shop, to see me, no doubt.

"I didn't realize you were such a fan of older women," I remarked to him as he walked into the donut shop.

"What are you talking about, Suzanne?"

"Actually, it's Ms. Hart while I'm on duty here at the donut shop. I'm sure you understand," I said, tweaking him a bit.

At least he had the sense to look embarrassed. "I'm sorry about that. I guess I was a little peeved about the chief naming Darby second-in-command, but right now, I'm glad I'm just a peon. I wouldn't want his headaches on a bet."

"It's not as easy as it looks, is it?" I asked, remembering when Phillip, my stepfather and the former April Springs chief of police, or even Jake, who had the job at one point as well, had been the chief in our parts.

"Not by a long shot. Can we bury the hatchet and go back to Rick and Suzanne?" he asked me sheepishly.

"Maybe. It depends on how you answer the next question," I told him.

He appeared to brace himself. "Go on. Ask it."

"How long have you been dating Karen Lexington on the side?"

His laughter caught everyone else's attention in the donut shop, and I felt my face redden slightly. "You've got it all wrong there, Suzanne."

"Don't try to deny it. I saw that hug and how intimately you just spoke with her," I insisted.

"She's my aunt. Ew, by the way."

"How did I not know that Karen was your aunt?" I asked him.

"I don't know. I didn't realize you were our local genealogist," he said with a smile. "Me and Aunt Karen? Seriously? I've got to tell you, it's kind of a relief hearing you pull something as boneheaded as that."

"Rick, if you're trying to get back in my good graces, you're going about it the wrong way," I warned him.

"I'm sorry. I just get so tired of hearing how you're a better cop than I'll ever be, it's nice to know that you're human too."

"Who says that?" I asked him, wondering how far my reputation as an amateur sleuth had preceded me.

"Now you're just asking to have your ego stroked, and that's way above my pay grade," he said with a smile as he offered his hand. "What do you say? Are we good?"

"We're good," I answered as I took it and gave him a firm shake. "Let me buy you a donut to seal the deal."

"The chief doesn't like us accepting gratuities," he said as he looked around the shop. After he'd laughed at me, when I'd scanned the room, everyone had made sure to focus their attention on their treats instead of us.

I grabbed a lemon-filled donut, which I knew was one of his favorites, and slid it across the counter as though it were some kind of contraband. "I won't tell if you won't."

The police officer looked clearly perplexed by the dilemma, and then he smiled. "I appreciate that," he said as he pulled a single dollar bill and stuffed it into Emma's tip jar.

"Well played, sir," I told him with a grin. "I'm guessing you all aren't making much headway in the investigation."

He shrugged as he answered. "I know the acting chief is keeping you in the loop, but that's his decision, not mine. No offense."

"None taken," I told him. "I'm guessing you didn't come by the shop hoping to spot your aunt on my doorstep, so what brings you by Donut Hearts?"

"I was sent to see if you had any idea when your husband might be coming home," he said.

"I'm guessing the acting chief sent you?" I asked him.

Officer Handler said softly, "Maybe yes, maybe no," as he nodded in agreement. "I'm not at liberty to disclose that."

"As far as I know, he and your boss won't be back for a few days. You should know, though, that it might even be longer than that. Chief Grant has a ton of vacation time saved up, and Grace usually burns most of hers helping me, so he's got a backlog he needs to knock down. As for Jake, he's going to take a bit of time off since he's been doing so much consulting lately. He needs to recharge his batteries too."

"Can't he do that with you?" Rick asked, and then he immediately realized how that must have sounded to me. "Strike that. I'm sorry, I don't know what I was thinking even asking that question."

"It's okay," I assured him. "Sure, he loves hanging out with me when he's off, but this chance was too good to pass up, and I urged him to take it. How about if I get you some coffee to go with that donut?"

"Thanks, but I've got the caffeine shakes as it is," Rick said. "Thanks for letting me off the hook, Suzanne."

"No worries, Rick. I'll see you later."

"There's no doubt about it in my mind," he said as he left Donut Hearts.

I was glad things were good between us again. I hated being at odds with any of my friends, and when I could fix things, so much the better.

Chapter 6

PROMPTLY AT ELEVEN, which was our normal closing time, Emma came out from the back without her apron. "The dishes are mostly finished, so is there any way I can get out of here early?"

"Sure," I said. "What's wrong, are you having more restaurant issues again?"

"No, but I've got a test at school I haven't studied for yet. It's in an hour, and I'm hoping I can cram enough into my tired brain to pass."

"You're not stretching yourself too thin, are you?" I asked her, more out of concern as her friend than her employer.

"What do you mean? Between working here with you, helping Mom and Barton set up the new restaurant, and going to college part-time, I've got at least five hours of free time every day."

"Isn't that when you should be sleeping?" I asked her with a grin.

"Sleep? What's that? I vaguely remember it, but I couldn't describe it to you on a bet. Don't worry, things should settle down soon."

As I let her out of the locked front door, I said, "You would think so, but other things have a way of coming up to take their places."

"Don't I know it," she answered. "Don't worry about me. Mom's been on me about that too. It's bad enough having one mother; I get two," she said as she hugged me spontaneously.

"Doesn't that just make you twice as lucky as most folks?" I laughed.

"In this case, it does. I'll see you tomorrow," Emma said as she buttoned up her coat on the way out.

"Not if I see you first," I answered with a grin.

Once she was gone, I started closing up for the day, running the register report, boxing up the extra donuts we had on hand, and finishing up the dishes in back. After the front and back were both shipshape, all I had left to do was finish sweeping, fill out the deposit, and then take it to the bank. Things had taken me a little longer than I'd expected, so I was surprised that I hadn't heard from Grace yet.

I was about to call her when my cell phone rang. "Hey, you," I said when I saw that it was the woman in question herself.

"Hi, Suzanne. I'm running a little late. Can I meet you there in half an hour?"

"You sound rushed. We can put it off longer than that if you need to," I told her.

"No, I've just got a new employee in my division, and you know how puppies can be. She's trying to change the world overnight, and I'm struggling to get her to realize that we do things the way we do for a reason. She'll tire herself out soon enough, but I'm going to be a bit late as things stand right now."

"Well, I won't be here by the time you finish up with her," I told her. "I'm on my way to the bank. Tell you what. I'm starving. Why don't you meet me at the Boxcar Grill after you're finished?"

"But then you'll finish eating before *I* get there," she protested.

"Hey, *I've* already put in a full day. A gal's got to eat if she's going to keep some meat on her bones, or so I've heard."

"Are you still letting that idiot's comment get to you? Suzanne, I *wish* I had your curves. I've always been jealous of your figure."

I thought about how trim and shapely my friend was. "Don't lie to me."

"I'm not," she protested.

"I know, but wow, would I ever love to have your shape instead of mine."

"We usually want whatever it is we don't have," Grace said with a sigh.

"Except for the men in our lives. We both got *exactly* what we wanted there."

"I agree. So, that makes it a win in that department at least. Tell you what," Grace added. "I'll see if I can get little Miss Robin squared away, and I'll be at the Boxcar before you get there, if I get lucky."

"Challenge accepted," I said with a grin.

"That wasn't a challenge, you big goofball," Grace answered in kind.

"Funny, but that's how *I* heard it. Sorry I can't keep talking, but I have to swing by the bank before I toast your buns."

"My buns will be just fine, thank you very much," Grace answered.

I could still hear her laughing as she hung up on me.

I decided to forego the extra sweeping I'd been considering, buttoned the place up, and raced for the bank. Knowing Grace, it was going to be a tight finish, but I would be dipped in corndog batter if I was just going to let her win.

The line at the bank had other plans for me, though.

I was waiting impatiently for the line to move when I heard someone sigh loudly behind me.

I turned around and found quite a surprise. "Vivian? How are you holding up?"

"I'm okay," she said as she stretched her neck a bit. "Why wouldn't I be?"

"Given what happened to Hal Embry last night, I just figured you'd be in mourning today too," I said. Karen had been wearing basic black when I'd seen her earlier, but Vivian was sporting a floral print dress that ended well above her knees.

"It was sad losing Hal that way, but life, like the show, must go on," she said, though she didn't really sound all that upset by the leading man's death to me.

"Did you happen to see anything backstage last night?" I asked, keeping my voice low. There were quite a few folks in the bank at the moment, and I didn't want any of them hearing me questioning a witness if I could help it.

"I saw a great many things," she said.

"I mean about what happened to Hal," I prodded her a bit.

"Suzanne, are you asking me if I saw anyone stab him, or perhaps if I did it myself?" she asked me softly. There was a snap to her tone, though she'd kept her volume down as well. Given what she'd just asked me, that didn't surprise me one bit.

"You can answer whichever question you'd like to first, but I want answers from you, not attitude," I said, giving her a hard look at the same time. I'd thought about trying to be a bit easier on her, but her attitude had set the stage for how I needed to proceed. If she wanted to be blunt about the whole thing, then I was determined to match her insolence with some of my own.

Vivian looked surprised by my statement for a second, and then she broke out into a smile. "Good for you. I didn't think you had the backbone to say something like that to me."

"What can I say? I'm just full of surprises some days. How about you?"

She shrugged. "I suppose that all depends on what you expect from me. Am I sad that someone stabbed Hal Embry with a knife on stage last night? I am. Surprised? Hardly. He was trying to play the three leading ladies off each other, so the only thing that really caught me off guard was how long it took someone to stop him."

That was quite a frank assessment. "I'm assuming you are including yourself as one of the leading ladies involved."

"I am. At least I was. I've suddenly lost my taste for the theater, so if and when that dreadful production resumes, they'll have to find someone else to play my role."

"So, you admit that you were having problems with Hal?" I asked her.

"Not as soon as I found out he was trying to play the three of us against each other," she said. "The other two ladies, and I use that term loosely, were more vested in replacing their lost husbands. I suppose that has more to do with being a widow than a divorcee. I understand the hard truth that *anyone* can be replaced, though I'm willing to admit that the pool shrinks with each passing moment. Men my age seem to drop dead at an alarming rate these days."

If Vivian was in mourning, she surely had an odd way of showing it. Then again, if she had murdered the aging ladies' man, she wasn't trying very hard to hide the animosity she felt toward him, either. "So, you believe that one of your fellow lead actors killed him?"

"I didn't say that, Suzanne. Not just them. Karen had her reasons as well, and so did Zane and Hillary."

"Zane I understand, since he was Hal's understudy, but why Hillary?" I asked her.

"You don't know? She made a play for him last year when we were doing *Love Lost in Youth*. He shot her down soundly, and she's been angry with him ever since. I don't know if you remember, but I absolutely *killed* in the role of Lola."

"Sorry, I didn't get a chance to see that one," I admitted.

"More's the pity," she answered. "Why Max felt the need to showcase Hal Embry is beyond me. I heard rumors, of course, but you never know what to believe."

"That Hal was financing the production?" I asked innocently.

"So, you're better at detecting than it might seem at first," she said. "I may be able to help you after all," she added with a wicked little grin. "If I were you, I'd speak with Geraldine Morgan."

"Why her and not Celia?"

"Celia is certainly a candidate, but I saw Hal say something to Geraldine before he sat down in his chair on stage last night, and her face turned the brightest shade of red. He clearly said something to her she didn't like."

"Did she go anywhere near him after that?" I asked her.

"How should I know? I was busy working on getting into character," she said. "Anyway, I just thought you might like to know that."

I was nearly at the front of the line, but I wasn't ready to stop questioning Vivian. "You can go ahead of me," I said as I fumbled with my deposit. It was perfect—I wouldn't have left Donut Hearts otherwise—but Vivian didn't need to know that.

"Are you sure?"

Was she reluctant to go ahead of me? "Positive," I said as I pretended to be frustrated by my lack of preparation. Vivian wasn't the only one who could act.

"Very well," she said as she took my place. I strained to hear the transaction, and I caught enough of it to wonder.

"How would you like this check cashed, ma'am?" the young teller asked Vivian.

"Twenties and tens, please," she said softly. That was the thing about her voice, though. It carried more than she might have intended.

The teller's eyebrows shot up. "Are you sure? That's going to make quite a stack of bills."

"Humor me," she said. "Hundreds are so difficult to cash on the road."

"Very well," the teller responded.

"Taking a trip?" I asked Vivian from over her shoulder.

Evidently, she'd forgotten all about me for the moment. "I thought I might," she said. "The only reason I was staying in town was for the play, and now that I'm dropping out, there's no reason I shouldn't start the trip I've been planning a bit earlier than I was expecting."

"I'd love to go somewhere myself," I said, which was true enough, even though my excursions often included murder. "Where are you headed?"

"Wherever the impulse leads me. I thought I'd get into my car and drive. It can be quite freeing to let the road dictate the destination," she said.

"Are you sure that's such a good idea?" I asked her gently.

"Why wouldn't it be?" Vivian asked me sharply.

"Leaving town so soon after a murder might make it look as though you're on the run," I told her. "Sometimes appearances can be incriminating."

"Not if I had nothing to do with the crime," she countered.

"Suit yourself," I said as the teller tried to jam a substantial number of bills into a banking envelope. She tore it as she tried, so she then shifted to a regular business-sized envelope. It still bulged from the large supply of cash, but at least she could get the flap partially closed.

"I always do," Vivian replied as she took the envelope and walked out of the bank.

What choice did I have? I gave up my place in line and followed her out of the building.

"What are you doing, Suzanne?" she asked me.

"We were having such a nice chat that I didn't want it to end," I said lamely.

"I'm sorry, but I have things to do before I'm ready to leave. I need to pack a few more things at home, and then I'm off."

"So, you're really going?" I asked her.

"I am," she said, dismissing me as she got into her Subaru Forester and drove away.

As I went back inside to start over in the line, I pulled out my phone and called Darby.

"What's up, Suzanne? Make it dance; I'm on hold on the other line."

"Well, if you don't do something fast, one of your suspects is going to flee your jurisdiction," I said, trying to make it sound more formal than my tip really was.

"Which suspect?"

"Vivian Crowe. She just cashed a pretty substantial check at the bank, and she told me she's heading out of town as soon as she can finish packing a few things at home."

"Blast it all, I told her to hang around not two hours ago," Darby said. "Is she in that Subaru of hers?"

"She is," I told him.

"Hang on." He put his hand over the phone, but I could still hear him. "Rick, go wrangle Vivian Crowe in at her place, would you? She's trying to ditch us. What? I don't know. Tell her if she doesn't cooperate, we'll have to start interviewing her neighbors and friends about her activities these past few weeks. No, of course we're not going to do that, but it should be enough of a bluff to get her to hang around for at least a few more days." He came back to me. "Okay, we're on it. Thanks for the tip."

"You bet. Who's on the other end of your phone call?" I asked, fishing a bit since I'd just given him a hot tip.

"Sorry. Gotta go," he said as he hung up on me.

Maybe he did, maybe he didn't. It appeared that the acting police chief was starting to get the hang of things after all.

I made it through the line again, and the teller raised an eyebrow at me as I slid the deposit across the desk to her.

"Weren't you just here?" she asked me as she worked.

"I thought I forgot something, but when I got outside, I realized that I was wrong," I said. It was the only lie I could think of on the spur of the moment.

The teller smiled gently at me as she handed me the slip. "Don't you worry a thing about it. It happens to my Nana all of the time."

I happened to know her Nana, and the fact that she was at least thirty years older than I was rankled me a bit, but I decided not to get into that at the moment.

If Grace had dealt with as much drama as I had, maybe I still had a chance of beating her to the Boxcar.

Chapter 7

I WALKED IN THROUGH the diner door and saw that I was too late. Not only was Grace already seated, but there was a dirty plate and an empty glass of tea sitting in front of her.

Exactly how long had I been held up at the bank, anyway?

"Sorry I'm late," I said as I took a seat across from her after blowing past the cash register up front. Trish was in back, waiting on a customer, so I waved to her as I sat down. "Thanks for waiting," I said sarcastically as I pointed to the dirty dishes.

"What can I say? I held out as long as I could, but the special is really great today. I highly recommend it," she said with a grin.

Trish joined us and grabbed one of the bins she used to clear the tables. "Is it okay with you if I clear the table now, Your Royal Highness?" she asked Grace. "Why in the world you would want someone else's dirty dishes in front of you is beyond me."

"You haven't already eaten?" I asked her.

"Don't believe anything she tells you. Grace got here two minutes ago," Trish said with a wry laugh. "What kind of weird game are you two playing today, and can I join in?" Her grin was infectious.

"Sorry, but it's over now," I told her. "We had a bet to see who could get here first, and evidently Grace won, but just barely."

"Hey, a win is a win in my book," Grace said.

"Just out of curiosity, what were the stakes?" Trish asked.

"Bragging rights, I guess," I conceded.

"Hey, don't discount those. Now, are you two lunatics ready to order?"

"What *is* today's special?" I asked her.

"Hilda made a baked ziti that's pretty amazing," Trish said loudly. In a softer voice, she said, "It's not up to Napoli's standards, but then again, what is? It's really pretty good, especially if you get one of her sourdough rolls to go along with it."

I thought about eating anything Italian that hadn't been made by Angelica or one of her daughters, and I just couldn't bring myself to do it. "That sounds great, but I'm more in the mood for a burger and fries today."

"Make it two," Grace said.

"I understand," Trish said. "Two sweet teas to go with them?"

"You know it," I said as I saw an old friend come in. "On second thought, you'd better make it three."

Trish looked over her shoulder. "Now what makes you think the mayor is going to want to have lunch with the likes of you two?" she asked me.

"One, we're a pair of nice-looking girls, and he could do a lot worse for lunch companions."

"Two," Grace continued, "he's going to want to talk to us about what happened at the theater last night."

"And three, and most importantly, there aren't any free tables available," I finished up.

"You two should take your act on the road sometime," Trish said with a laugh.

"We would, but then we'd end up missing you," I told her.

"No doubt," she said as the mayor hovered near our table.

"Room for one more, ladies?" George Morris asked. The three of us burst out laughing, which made the mayor frown. "What's so funny? Was it something I said?"

"No, sir. It's an inside joke that really isn't all that amusing. Please, have a seat."

"If I'm going to be in the way..." he started to say before I could cut him off.

"George, we were laughing at ourselves, not you. Join us. I've got good news. They have a baked ziti on the menu for lunch."

George shrugged. "That sounds good." It was clear that he didn't believe it, but he was doing his best to present it that way.

Trish smacked him with her order pad. "You can forget all about that, mister. There's no way I'm serving Angelica DeAngelis's boyfriend *anything* Italian. The girls are having burgers. You want one too?"

"Please," he said, looking much relieved. "If I go over there later with oregano on my breath, there's going to be all kinds of trouble I don't need."

"I totally get that," Trish answered as she left to get our drinks.

"How is that going, Mr. Mayor?" I asked George with a grin. "You two looked like you belonged on top of a wedding cake last night at the theater."

"Any plans in that direction?" Grace asked him with a smile of her own.

"No," he said flatly. "And I've been told in no uncertain terms not to bring it up again."

He said it with a sad finality that made me sorry that we'd been teasing him so hard. "You didn't ask her already, did you?"

"I was getting around to it, but she shut me down before I could even get down on one knee," he admitted. "She loves me, and I love her. I don't know what I did so wrong that she doesn't want to marry me."

"Is it just to you, or to *anybody*?" I asked him earnestly.

"I didn't realize anyone else was getting ready to propose to her, Suzanne. Do you know something I don't?"

"Just that Angelica had a bad time of her first marriage, no matter that she got four wonderful daughters from the union," I told him. "If things aren't broke, why try to fix them?"

"Blast it, woman, I'm in love. Is it so wrong that I want to spend the rest of my life with her? I didn't think so, but apparently she does."

"Give her some time, George," I urged him. "She'll come around. Just make sure that you're still able and willing when she is ready."

"There's no danger of that," he said. "I'm absolutely smitten by the woman."

"And why shouldn't you be?" Grace asked him. "She's pretty amazing."

"She is, but then again, so is George," I said, defending His Honor.

"I never said that he wasn't," Grace retorted.

The conversation died when Trish arrived with our food. As we ate, there wasn't a great deal of time to talk about much other than how good the burgers and fries were. I'd been expecting George to bring up the murder at the theater the night before, but he kept the tone light, which was fine with me. I'd been known to discuss homicide over a meal, but it wasn't always my first choice of dining topics.

Once we were finished eating, George sat back in his chair and smiled. "If either one of you ever repeats this, I'll deny it and call you both liars, but sometimes all I really need is one of Trish's burgers and fries."

"Hey, we get it, and what's more, we agree," I said, not wanting to poke or prod our friend any more than we already had.

The mayor waved to Trish for the check, and she brought over three separate ones.

"I'll cover those," George said as he reached for them.

"*I* was going to treat us," Grace pouted.

"Tell you what. Why don't we all pay for our *own* meals? How does that sound? That way there's no hard feelings," I said.

"And you get out of offering to buy us both lunch," Grace said as she looked over at George.

"I'm *more* than happy to pay," I said in frustration, and then I saw both of them grinning at me. "Did you two plan this little skit of yours ahead of time?"

"No, we just made it up on the spot," Grace said with a chuckle as she gave the mayor a high five, which he gleefully returned.

I was about to stand when George asked, "Do you two have a second before you rush off to solve Hal Embry's murder?"

"What makes you think we're going to do that?" I asked him, being as coy as I could manage. Unfortunately, the man knew me too well.

"Suzanne, if you two aren't in this investigation up to your eyebrows, I'll buy you both lunch for the rest of the year," George said. When we didn't deny it, he smiled gently. "That's what I thought. Have you made any progress?"

"A little," I admitted. "It just happened last night, as you well know. I've been working all morning, and so has Grace. We're heading out now to see if we can track down any more of our suspects. I've already talked to Karen Lexington. She came by the donut shop this morning, declaring her innocence for all of the world to hear."

"And we interviewed Max and Hillary Teal for some background information last night," Grace added.

"Well, I for one hope you solve this one quickly," he said. "With Jake and Stephen out of town, I'm afraid Darby has a bit much on his plate." Before we could protest, if we were even going to, he quickly added, "Don't get me wrong. He's perfectly qualified for the job, but it can't be easy. Besides, this is a black mark on April Springs. We need to figure this out, and fast."

"*We*?" I asked him pointedly. "I thought you gave up investigating crime when you retired from helping me."

"Let's just say that I'm ready and available to step in if you need me. It's a shame Phillip is gone too."

"He's not in town? What are you talking about?" I asked the mayor, surprised to hear the news about my stepfather.

"Stephen invited him to the cabin this morning," he said. "I'm surprised you didn't hear about it. Would you believe that? I know something the great Suzanne Hart doesn't."

His smile was broad, and I wasn't about to take it from him. "I'm sure the things you know that I don't would fill an ocean, Mr. Mayor."

"Hey, I was just kidding," he said quickly, sensing my tone.

"Easy, George, she's just getting you back for that joke earlier."

"If that's the case, she hasn't done anything yet to you," George pointed out.

"Why do you think I'm sitting here quivering in my seat? I know it's coming. I just don't know when or exactly how."

"If you two are finished, we need to go, Grace," I said as I stood. "It was nice having lunch with you, Mayor. And remember. You need to hang in there. Angelica is worth waiting for."

"You don't have to tell me that," he said. "Happy hunting, ladies."

After we paid our tabs, splitting the bill three ways as I'd suggested, Grace looked at me expectantly out in front of the Boxcar Grill. "So, where do we head first?"

As we walked over to my Jeep, I said, "Thanks to Max, Celia is willing to speak to us today, so why don't we go to Maple Hollow first?"

"That sounds good to me," Grace said as we got in and I headed us in that direction.

"Should we call her first before we waste a trip?" I asked.

"I'm not entirely sure we should let her know we're coming. I'd kind of like to catch her off guard," Grace replied.

"What if she's not home though?" I asked.

"That's a fair point. What do you think? I'll leave it up to you."

"Call her. It's better to be safe than sorry."

Grace pondered my answer for a moment, and then she reached for her phone. "Hand me that card she gave you last night."

I reached for my slim wallet and gave the entire thing to her. "It's in there somewhere."

Grace didn't take it immediately. "Are you sure you want me doing that? I'd hate to invade your privacy."

I had to laugh. "I'm not exactly sure how you could do that, since you know everything there is to know about me. If there's something in there that you *aren't* aware of, it would shock me to my toes."

"Okay, but don't say I didn't warn you," she said.

Digging out Celia's card took longer than it should have, and when I looked over, I saw that Grace was frowning. "What's wrong? Isn't it in there?"

"It is, but I found something else a lot more troubling than a business card," she said softly.

What on earth could she be talking about? "I have no idea what it is, but there's nothing I have to be ashamed of."

"Not even this?" she asked as she held up a long-defunct Blockbuster Video card. "Why are you still carrying this around with you?"

"As a form of ID?" I asked her with a shrug.

"Try again."

"I forgot it was in there," I admitted.

"Do I have your permission to toss it?" she asked me.

"I don't know, I've kind of gotten used to having it," I said.

"Well, sometimes change is hard," she said as she put it in her purse.

"Yeah, you're right," I said. "Thanks. I don't know, but I could never bring myself to do it for some odd reason."

"Hey, if I had to justify every quirk of mine, I'd never get anything else done," she answered. "I could always put it back if you'd rather."

I thought about it for a second, and then I shook my head. "No, you're right. Besides, that will make room for my Junior Detective ID card I got from a cereal box last week."

"Ooh, I want one too," she said with a smile.

"Sorry, but you have to have special qualifications to get one."

"I'm a good investigator too," she protested.

"I know you are, but that's not what you need. You've got to send in ten box tops and proof of purchases for KABOOM KAPOW cereal."

"Do you actually eat that stuff?" she asked me with a frown.

"No, but one of my young customers does, and she thought it would be a hoot to get an ID card for me," I answered with a grin.

"Wow, we really are famous, aren't we?" Grace asked with a laugh.

"Why wouldn't we be?" I asked in return.

Grace used Celia's calling card and dialed the number on it. She put the phone on speaker so I could listen in, and when the woman in question answered, Grace asked, "Celia? It's Grace Gauge. Suzanne Hart and I are on our way to see you and talk to you about last night."

"I'm sorry. *Who* exactly are you again? Are you with the police?" She sounded as though she had never heard of us.

"We're Max's ex-wife and her best friend," Grace explained.

"Oh, yes. That. I'm sorry, but after reflecting a bit on the situation, I realize that I have nothing to share with you."

I was about to say something when Grace held up her free hand. "We understand. It's a shame, though. Max is going to be so disappointed when he finds out you wouldn't even meet with us, especially since we drove all the way to Maple Hollow."

We were nowhere near the town, but I wasn't about to point that out.

After a moment's hesitation, Celia said, "Oh, very well. I'm afraid I'm tied up at the moment. Would it be a terrible imposition to call me back in an hour?"

That would give us time to drive there and hunt down her address, so I nodded.

Grace sighed audibly. "I suppose we can make that work."

"I might be able to rush things a bit," the amateur actress said.

I shook my head, and Grace answered her, "No, that's fine. We wouldn't want to inconvenience you. We'll see you in an hour." She hung up, thereby keeping Celia from countering with an earlier time that we probably wouldn't be able to hit.

"You're a bad, bad girl. You know that, right?" I asked with a laugh.

"Hey, I do what I can," she said. "Do you think someone's there with her, or does she just really not want to talk to us?"

"I don't know. I kind of wish we were in town so we could stake her place out."

"Maybe I shouldn't have called after all," Grace admitted.

"No, it was the right thing to do. I wonder why she's had a change of heart. Is it possible that someone's already gotten to her?"

"If I've learned anything working with you, Suzanne, it's that anything's possible," Grace replied.

"It's kind of inconvenient having our suspects spread out over three towns," I told her. "I can see us putting some miles on my Jeep before we solve this thing."

"Sorry," she said. "I'd offer to drive my company car, but they're really starting to crack down on us after Nancy Benton wrecked her Lexus at the beach when she was supposed to be on a sales call in Charlotte."

"Did they fire her?" I asked.

"No, Nancy caters to some pretty big clients, and they all love her. Instead of reprimanding her, they put limits on all of the rest of us. What happened to the good old days? When you messed up, *you* were the only one who suffered the consequences? Everyone's so scared of their shadows these days that they punish *everyone* to keep from having to discipline the one *guilty* person."

"I wouldn't know about that," I told her honestly. "That's one of the advantages of me being my own boss."

"Don't feel *too* smug about it," Grace replied with a grin. "You don't get a company car, paid vacation, a healthy 401(k), or health or dental insurance, either. Need I go on?"

"So what you're saying is that there are advantages and disadvantages to both of our situations," I said with a laugh.

"Exactly."

"Good to know."

Unfortunately, by the time we got to the address on Celia Laslow's card, she was already gone.

Chapter 8

I'D BEEN HOPING TO save us a trip to Maple Hollow if Celia hadn't been available, but evidently, our phone call had given her time to change her mind yet again and take off before we could get there. Grace had been right. It was worth a few wasted trips if we could catch someone doing something they shouldn't be doing, and I told her exactly that as we walked up the front steps of her house, even though there were no cars in sight in her driveway.

"Don't worry about it, Suzanne," she said after I apologized.

"From now on, we'll keep our next move to ourselves," I said.

"That sounds like a plan to me."

"What's that?" Grace asked me as I plucked off a folded piece of paper that had been taped to the door.

"I don't know, but I doubt that it's good news," I told her.

Ladies,

Had to go be with a friend. Hope you understand.

Celia.

"So we made plans to see her and she bugged out on us instead," Grace said unhappily.

"So much for courtesy calls," I said as I started to crumple the note up.

"Don't do that," Grace said as she grabbed it and folded it back up. "I want to use it as evidence in the trial."

I looked at her in surprise. "Do you honestly think this is some kind of admission of guilt?"

"No, I'm talking about my assault trial when I see her again," Grace answered.

"Now, Grace, you know we can't go around hitting people, no matter how much they might deserve it," I said with a slight smile.

"You're right, but a girl can dream, can't she? Where does that leave us?"

"Well, we don't have any other suspects in Maple Hollow, so we might as well go back to April Springs and see if we can find any of the other folks on our list," I told her.

"But we aren't going to warn them first that we're coming, right?" she asked.

"Right."

"Good enough," Grace replied as we got back into my Jeep and headed home.

When we neared town, Grace asked, "Which one should we tackle first, Vivian or Zane?"

"I say Vivian is the more likely of the two," I told her, "but my judgment today is evidently not all that sound. You decide."

"Suzanne, that's water over the bridge, or under the dam, or wherever it goes when we're finished with it. Vivian is the right choice."

"I appreciate that," I said as we drove to Vivian Crowe's place.

No one was home there either, and again there wasn't a car in the driveway. "I'm beginning to get a little paranoid," Grace said. "Where *is* everyone?"

"I can't imagine that they're *all* ducking us," I said as I sat there wondering what to do next.

"I don't see why not," she answered. "We're getting to be known in the area for digging things up that folks don't want exposed. Is this going to be the way it goes from now on? Have we completely lost the element of surprise?"

"Maybe, but I'm not giving up just yet," I told her.

"Then let's go find Zane Whitlow."

Zane was home, but there was an extra car in his driveway. What was more, it was one I recognized.

Apparently Hillary Teal was paying the understudy a visit herself, but I had a feeling that it had nothing to do with our investigation into Hal Embry's death.

I started to knock on the door when Grace grabbed my hand. "What's going on?"

"Listen. Did you hear that?" she asked softly.

"Hear what?"

"Shhh," she told me, and I tried to hear what had gotten her attention.

Whatever she'd heard was lost on me. "I don't hear anything. What was it?" I asked.

Before she could answer, the front door shot open, and Hillary Teal came rushing out, clearly unhappy about something.

"What on earth are you two doing here?" she asked as her breathing quickened.

"We wanted to talk to Zane about last night," I said.

"How about you? What brings you by?" Grace asked her innocently. I could see her suppressing a smile, and I had to look away. If she started grinning, I wouldn't be able to stop myself, and that wouldn't be very productive as far as our investigation was concerned.

"We were just talking!" she said, the words spilling out of her in a rush. "He was upset, and I was trying to comfort him."

"That was sweet of you," Grace said.

"Well, we do what we can for those in need," Hillary said as she brushed past us and headed toward her car. "Ladies."

"Bye," I answered in kind as Zane came outside to join us on the front stoop.

"May I help you, ladies?" he asked us politely.

"You may," I said. "We're here to talk about what happened last night."

"I'm sorry, but I'm going to be late for work if I don't leave this instant," Zane replied as he shut the door behind him and headed for his car. It hadn't taken Hillary long to scoot, and evidently, Zane wasn't going to be far behind her.

"It will just take a second," Grace said, trying to block his way.

"Unfortunately, it's a second I don't have," he replied. "Besides, I've got nothing to say. I didn't see anything out of the ordinary last night."

Zane clearly meant it to be dismissive, but I wasn't going to let that happen. "We can meet you after work if you'd prefer, but we need to speak with you."

The understudy must have read the hard tone of my voice, because he shrugged as he got into his car and started the engine. "Fine. If it's that important for you to talk to me, I'll be back at eight," he answered.

"Morning or evening?" Grace asked him with a sweet smile.

"Evening," he said gruffly. "That visit from Hillary was nothing significant, so don't go getting any ideas or spreading any rumors."

"We wouldn't dream of it," I answered. "See you tonight."

After he was gone, Grace looked at me and smiled. "Suzanne, do you think there is a possibility that they were actually in there canoodling?"

"Hey, they're senior citizens, they aren't dead," I said. "If they were, then I say good for her. She went after what she wanted."

"And it appears that she may just have gotten it, no matter how much Zane may have protested to the contrary," Grace replied. "Now I'm definitely getting paranoid. We're going to have to start wearing disguises to even get people to talk to us if this keeps up."

"I know we're getting shut out, but we can't stop trying. What do you say? Do you feel like a drive to Union Square?"

"I wish I could come up with a reason to say no, but I can't. Let's go give Geraldine Morgan a chance to ignore us too."

I stopped the car a hundred feet from Geraldine Morgan's place. "What happened? Did your Jeep break down?" Grace asked me.

"This thing is perfectly reliable," I told her as I patted the steering wheel. "I haven't had a drop of trouble out of it since I bought it."

"Yeah, but don't forget. You totaled the last one," she said. "So, if we aren't having mechanical trouble, why are we stopping?"

"Look up there," I said as I pointed to where Geraldine lived, based on our directions.

"Is that Celia with her on the front porch?" Grace asked me.

"It surely seems that way to me. Come on. Let's see how close we can get and see if we can hear what they're talking about," I said as I opened the door and got out.

Grace followed suit, and we started toward them.

I heard Celia say, "Geraldine, we have to tell someone."

Geraldine answered frostily, "We can't, and you know it."

"I know nothing of the sort," Celia countered.

Geraldine was about to answer when a dog suddenly appeared out of nowhere beside us, safely behind a chain link fence but aggressive nonetheless. It started barking in an agitated manner, apparently dying to get at us. Of course that caught the attention of the two older actresses. So much for our lurking, spying, and subterfuge.

"We're busted," I whispered to Grace as I started walking quickly toward Geraldine's house. I waved brightly and put on my best smile as I said, "Hi, ladies. I'm so glad we found you!"

"Suzanne Hart, what are you doing here?" Celia asked angrily as we approached. "Have you been following me?"

"Honestly, Grace and I are shocked that you're here," I told her, which was truthful enough. "I thought you said that you had to go be with a friend. Is that why you ditched us?"

Celia didn't even flinch as she started to spin out an excuse. "I told you before that I didn't have anything to add to the conversation, and Geraldine and I needed to talk."

"So we heard as we were walking up," Grace said.

It was one way to go, maybe not the direction I would have chosen, but now that we were committed, it was time to bluff a bit. "You really shouldn't keep things from us *or* the police," I said, venturing a guess as to what they might have been discussing before that yard dog so rudely interrupted our eavesdropping.

"What on earth are you talking about?" Geraldine asked me icily.

"Come on, you're among friends here," Grace said.

"I sincerely doubt that," Celia answered.

"You might as well tell us what you know," I said calmly. "We can help you."

Celia was clearly wavering, but Geraldine took her hand and squeezed it tightly enough to make Celia's fingers whiten. "We were just discussing the fact that we need to tell Max he should cancel the show out of respect to Hal's memory."

"That's right," Celia said haltingly. "That's all."

I wanted to say "Liar, liar, pants on fire," but that wouldn't have done any of us any good. "We really are the good guys here," I replied.

"Unless the two of you are helping shield a killer," Grace added. "If that's the case, we'll do everything in our power to make sure that you are both prosecuted to the fullest extent of the law."

I thought that sounded a little harsh.

"We have nothing to say," Geraldine intoned. "Now if you'll excuse us, Celia and I have plans to make."

"Are you going on a trip together? Vivian already tried that, and the police are making her stay," I told them, wondering if even more suspects were trying to get away from the investigation. That was one problem when most of our suspects were beyond retirement age. They didn't have any compelling reason to hang around.

"No, of course not. We're planning a wake for poor dear Hal," Geraldine said haughtily.

"Wouldn't that be Karen Lexington's job?" Grace asked her.

Geraldine discounted her rival with a sweep of her hand. "She can do as she sees fit, but *we* are going to conduct a fond farewell with the only people who really mattered to Hal, his theater group family."

That should be interesting to see. "If that's the case, then we'd love to pay our respects as well," I said.

"Suzanne can cater the affair, since Hal loved donuts so much," Grace volunteered.

It was quite a stretch to make that particular claim, but who was I to disagree with her?

"Suzanne? Would you really do that?" Celia asked. "We can't afford to pay you for them, but it would be lovely of you to provide them gratis, in honor of the dearly departed."

"Of course," I replied, biting my lower lip first. "I'd be honored to help out. When is this memorial going to occur?"

"Tomorrow," Geraldine said decisively.

"Before there's even a funeral?" Celia asked, clearly surprised by the timing as well.

"We don't want to interfere with anyone else's plans," Geraldine said. "Now come inside. We have plans to make."

I started to follow them when Geraldine stopped in her tracks and turned to face me. "I'm sure you understand, but this is something we need to do alone. I believe twelve dozen donuts should be sufficient for the event. We'll see you tomorrow at the theater at three."

"Twelve dozen donuts? Does she honestly believe that one hundred and forty-four people are going to come mourn Hal Embry? Even if they each take two, that's still seventy-two mourners," I told Grace after the two senior women were gone. "Thanks for volunteering my services, by the way."

"It was the only way we were going to get an invitation," she said. "If you'd like, I'll cover your costs."

"I may have to take you up on it," I told her. "Things have been a little slow at the shop lately. There's no way I'm making twelve dozen donuts after working a full morning, though."

"Eight dozen maybe?" Grace asked.

"I can do that, even if everybody who comes has three or four apiece *and* takes some home with them to boot," I replied. "Still, that's a lot more doable. Celia clearly wanted to tell us something, but Geraldine's got some kind of hold over her, doesn't she?"

"She must, because they surely weren't talking about a wake when we overheard them. What do you suppose they were really discussing?" Grace asked.

"I don't know, but we need to call Darby and let him know that something's going on between the two of them."

"We should invite him to the service too," Grace said.

"He needs to be there," I agreed, "but are you sure we're the ones who should tell him?"

"Well, I wouldn't hold my breath waiting for either one of *them* to do it," Grace said as she gestured back toward the closed door.

"Don't worry, I won't," I said as my phone rang. I was hoping for Jake, but I was almost as happy to see that Momma was calling me instead.

"Hey there, what's up?" I asked her as I held a finger up to Grace.

"Is that how you always answer the telephone, Suzanne?" Momma chided me.

"No, sometimes I just start giggling until the other person says something first," I told her.

"Is that true?" she asked me incredulously.

"Not even a little bit. Hello, Mother. How are you?"

"I'm fine, thank you for asking," she said, the automatic reply cued up and waiting to be delivered. "And you?"

"Just peachy keen," I said. "Now can I inquire as to the reason for this call, not that I don't enjoy hearing your delightful voice."

"Is that supposed to be me?" she asked.

"Why, did it ring any bells?" I asked, laughing a bit as I did. It was dicey making fun of her that way, but hey, sometimes it's fun to live on the edge.

"I suppose it did," she said, and then she rewarded me with a slight chuckle. "Do you have any dinner plans this evening?"

"Grace and I will probably grab something out," I said as I looked at my friend inquiringly. She nodded in agreement.

"Why don't you both come eat with me? With our spouses all out of town, it might be nice to have a bit of company."

Did Momma sound the slightest bit lonely as she made the invitation? I had been about to suggest to Grace that we go to Napoli's since we were already in Union Square, even though it was still a few hours until dinnertime, but I couldn't leave Momma alone to fend for herself. Nor could I give in too easily either, though, or she'd suspect we would join her out of pity. What a complicated dance existed between my mother and me, even all these years later. "That depends. What are you serving?"

"Pot roast, baby carrots, new potatoes, and pearl onions," she said. "Does that meet with your satisfaction?"

"Is there any chance you have some homemade bread too?" I asked, pushing my luck.

"I suppose I could defrost a loaf," she said evenly. "Does that suit Your Highness?"

"It does," I said with a grin. "That sounds magnificent. Thanks for inviting us, Momma," I added warmly.

"You know that you are *always* welcome at my table," she said, pleased with my declaration of appreciation. "Do you need to ask Grace first?"

"Hang on," I said, not bothering to mute or even put my phone to my chest. "Grace, Momma just offered to feed us pot roast with all the trimmings. What do you say?"

"I say what are we doing standing here?" Grace asked with a grin. As a kid, she'd had nearly as many meals at my house as I had, so she was well acquainted with my mother's delightful cooking.

"That was hardly a formal invitation," Momma said when I got back on the line with her.

"Since when did Grace need a formal invitation, or me either, for that matter?" I asked her. "See you in a few hours. When is a good time for you?"

"It will be ready at four, but it won't hurt to simmer," she said.

"Four it is then," I said, and then I hung up before she had a chance to protest. Given my work hours, I loved an early dinner, and I knew that Grace was pretty adaptable. "That was fun," I told her as I put my phone away.

"One of these days, you're going to push her too far," Grace replied.

"One of these days? I've done it before, and I'm sure that I'll do it again," I told her. "Sorry about that."

"About what?" she asked, clearly confused by my apology.

"I was going to suggest a snack at Napoli's, but that's not going to work now."

"There's always tomorrow," she said with a grin.

"Are you kidding? After I finish closing the shop for the day, I have to start making that second round of donuts." I frowned at her, but she could see the smile in my eyes.

"I'll help out in the kitchen if you'd like me to," she replied.

"Thanks, but I'm good. It's going to cut into our investigation a bit though," I answered as we got into my Jeep and headed back to April Springs.

"It's worth it, in my opinion," she said as she took out her phone.

"Who are you calling now?" I asked.

"Darby needs us to update him, remember?" she asked.

"Put it on speaker. Maybe we can get lucky and sneak in a few questions of our own while we have him on the phone."

"Suzanne Hart, ever the dreamer," Grace said, and then she did as I'd asked.

Chapter 9

"WHAT'S UP, LADIES?" Darby asked as a response to our telephone call.

"How do you know we're both on the line?" I asked him.

"Call it an educated guess. Why, was I wrong?" he asked.

"That's beside the point."

"I figured that if I got one of you, I'd get the other too. Was that why you called, to check on the way I answer my phone?"

"We have news," Grace said. "As promised, we're keeping you in the loop."

"I could use some news. Is it good or bad?" Darby asked. It was clear he wasn't having as much luck with his investigation as he'd hoped.

"Good, I believe. There's going to be a wake tomorrow at three for Hal Embry at the auditorium, and unless I miss my guess, all of your suspects will be there," I told him.

"How did you two manage to get yourselves invited?" he asked me.

"It turns out that I'm catering the soiree, free of charge," I told him.

"That was awfully generous of you."

"Don't thank me, thank Grace. She's the one who made the offer." I stuck my tongue out at her, something the acting chief of police couldn't see.

"Hey, I'm buying the supplies," she protested.

"Then it's nice of both of you. How do I figure in?" Darby asked.

"You could help us with the boxes of donuts," I suggested. "Or if that sounds like too much work, we can let you in through the back door, and you can lurk in the wings and eavesdrop."

"Let me think about it," Darby answered.

"Seriously? Darby, you *have* to be there. You know that, don't you?" Grace asked him.

"Of course I do. I'm just not sure how I'm going to go about not being spotted while I'm sneaking in. If they see a uniform, they might not speak so freely. I'll let you know one way or the other how I want to go about it tomorrow. Thanks for thinking of me," he added.

"You're most welcome," I said as sweetly as I could manage. "Is there anything that you'd like to share with us while we have you on the line?"

He paused so long that I had to wonder if we'd lost the connection before he finally spoke.

"We've eliminated a few suspects that weren't actually associated with the play," he said. "It turns out that Max is a stickler for who gets to be backstage during one of his plays, even his rehearsals," Darby said.

"Was there anyone in particular you were looking at?" I asked him. He was being thorough; I had to give him credit for that.

"Hal didn't get along with his late wife's sister, but she's got a rock-solid alibi. She was in Virginia with her husband and his family. There's no way she could have done it."

"That's good to know," Grace said. "Anyone else?"

"Until this play, Hal led a pretty mild time of it since he retired."

"Was there any bad blood with old business partners?" I asked on a whim.

"As a matter of fact, there was. He ran a bowling alley with his childhood friend, a man named Danny Newburg, and three years ago, the two had a falling out that was pretty bad, from what I gather."

"What's his alibi?" Grace asked.

"It's airtight. The man's been dead eighteen months," Darby replied.

"So that would make it tough for him to kill Hal," I said.

Nobody got my sarcasm. Wow, sometimes people just didn't understand my skewed sense of humor.

"Anyway," Darby filled in, "I'm feeling as though you two are on the right track. It's got to be related to the theater somehow. I'll come by the donut shop tomorrow afternoon, and we'll work out the logistics."

"Sounds good, but you don't have to be a stranger until then. Feel free to keep in touch if anything comes up in the meantime."

"Right back at you," Darby said, and then he ended the call.

"Seriously, Suzanne? You're joking about the situation we're in?" Grace asked me as soon as she put her telephone away.

"What can I say? It's tough to just turn on and off," I answered.

"Try," she said, and then she smiled at me, taking the sting out of her criticism.

"I'll do my best, just because you're the one who is asking."

"Ladies, I hope you're hungry," Momma said as we walked into her cottage a few minutes before four. The aromas from dinner were amazing, and there was another layer I hadn't been expecting.

"Is that your apple pie?" I asked her eagerly.

"Actually, it's for all of us," Momma said, smiling softly.

"Now I see where you get your sense of humor," Grace replied.

"So then it's not my fault," I told her.

"I wouldn't say that," she answered.

"What are you two talking about?" Momma asked me. "Actually, I withdraw the question. Let's eat. It's sheer torture smelling that pot roast and not being able to have some."

"You could have gone ahead without us," I told her as Grace and I took turns washing up.

"Nonsense."

"I don't know how you managed it, Dot," Grace told her, "but I'm glad you did."

As we sat at the table, Momma passed around a platter overflowing with tender roast and perfectly done vegetables. After I loaded up my plate, I looked around and frowned. "I was told that there would be bread."

"It's coming," she said.

"Stay right where you are. I'll grab it," Grace answered.

"Thank you, dear," Momma replied with a smile.

"You always were her favorite," I said, giving Grace a snotty look that she knew I didn't mean.

"Now, girls, you're both pretty," Momma responded.

"I think all three of us are rather fetching." I laughed.

As we ate that wonderful meal, I found myself reveling in the love I was surrounded with as well as the food. These were my two favorite ladies in the world, bar none, and it was an honor to share a meal with them. "That was amazing," I told her as I chased the last small bite of carrot with my fork.

"I hope you saved some room," Momma said. "The pie should be cool enough to eat by now."

"Is there any chance there's vanilla ice cream too?" Grace asked.

"I wouldn't dream of serving pie without it," Momma replied.

"Oh, goody." She sounded like a twelve-year-old, and it made me laugh. "You like ice cream with your pie too," Grace chided me.

"I do indeed," I agreed. "I just wish our men knew what they were missing. I imagine they're sitting around the campfire, sharing beans from a can, while we're eating like royalty."

"Actually, Phillip is trying out his new smoker," Momma said. "They're having baby back ribs tonight."

"Hush and let me have my own version of reality," I told her as I got up and helped dish out the ice cream over the slices of pie Momma prepared.

"You can keep all your double-crust pies, as far as I'm concerned," I said after the first bite. "A crumb topping is the only way to go."

"Agreed," Momma said.

"Don't you think so too, Grace?" I asked her.

"Hey, I nodded, but I wasn't about to stop eating to do something as mundane as talking about it," she said.

"You always were the smart one," I said with a chuckle.

"Beauty *and* brains," she agreed, and then we all started laughing again.

As we cleaned up the dishes, Momma asked, "So, how goes the investigation?"

I didn't even bother trying to deny it, since my mother knew us both too well. "It's frustrating at the moment. Our suspects are either ducking us completely, or they aren't telling us anything close to the truth about the case," I admitted.

"You can't let that stop you," Momma said.

"Do you honestly feel that way?" I asked her. "I didn't think you liked us meddling in murder."

"I don't, but Hal Embry deserves justice," Momma answered.

"Did you know him well?" Grace asked her.

"Once upon a time, he tried to court me," Momma said, something that I had no idea about until that very moment.

"You're kidding, right?" I asked her.

"Suzanne, you might not be able to tell now, but I used to be considered quite fetching."

"I don't doubt it for a second, since I think you're still beautiful," I responded quickly. "But Hal? Come on. What chance did he stand?"

"Against your father? Very little. But he was persistent; I'll give him that."

"How did Dad respond to that?" I asked, curious to hear details about my long-gone father, especially in that light.

"Actually, it spurred him on to propose to me," Momma said with a slight smile. "I never actually thanked Hal for that appropriately, so I'll be happy if you can find his killer as a way of paying tribute to him."

"What was he like back then?" I asked.

"Well, he was thin and had the waviest brown hair I'd ever seen on anyone, man or woman. He could be quite the ladies' man when he put his mind to it," Momma said.

I tried to reconcile that with the man I'd seen murdered, and I had a hard time doing it. "So his behavior lately wasn't completely out of character," I mused.

"You know my opinion. As folks age, most of them don't really change. It's just that their true selves show themselves more and more. Some folks seem to get nicer, and some just the opposite, but I don't think there are any magical transitions going on. They just lose their ability to disguise their true selves anymore."

"I don't know if that's cynical or just realistic," Grace mused as she worked at drying the dishes as I washed them. Momma kept putting things away as we worked, since she was the only one of us who knew where everything went.

"It's just the way things are," Momma said.

"Do you know the three tarts?" I asked her.

Momma looked surprised by my description. "Three tarts?"

"That's what we've been calling Hal's leading ladies. That or the three merry widows," I explained unapologetically. "I'm talking about Celia Laslow, Geraldine Morgan, and Vivian Crowe."

Momma tried to hide her smile but failed to do so. "I suppose that tart is as good a designation as any. I take it they are all suspects?"

"They are, along with Zane Whitlow, Karen Lexington, and Hillary Teal," Grace added.

"My, they're *all* of my generation, aren't they," she said.

"That's why we need any insights you might have into them," I said. Why hadn't we come to Momma the very first thing? She was one of the sharpest evaluators of folks I knew, and these people were all in her age range. I felt like an idiot ignoring such a valuable resource. Thank goodness my greed for her great food had brought me to her doorstep during our investigation, even if it was solely by accident.

"I've run into all of them over the years," Momma admitted. "Goodness, do you honestly believe that so many of them could have a motive to kill poor Hal?"

"We do," I admitted. "Karen was his spurned girlfriend, the tarts wanted his affection too, which apparently he was more than happy to provide, Zane was his rival for the play's lead role, and Hillary was extremely overprotective of Zane."

"Are they an item?" Momma asked me, surprised by the inference.

"If they aren't at the moment, they might soon be. We caught them together this afternoon, and Hillary seemed to be a bit flustered by us finding her there," Grace said with a grin.

"My, my, my. I knew Hillary had feelings for him, but I never thought she'd act on them," Momma answered.

"Nobody's getting any younger, especially in that group," I said.

"Suzanne, they are all close to my own age, as you so recently admitted."

"Maybe chronologically, but you're MUCH younger in attitude," I said truthfully.

Grace grinned at us both. "You've got to admit, Dot, your daughter has a way of squirming out of most of the uncomfortable situations she causes."

"It's a real gift," Momma agreed.

"I prefer to think of it as a knack, but I'll take it," I told them both archly.

We all laughed at that, and then Grace asked, "What do you know about the three...lead actresses?"

"Oh, let's go on and continue calling them tarts," Momma conceded. "The name's as good as any. Celia trapped her first husband into marrying her by claiming a false pregnancy, Geraldine stole Vivian's fiancé a week before the wedding, and in retaliation, Vivian stole Freddie right back on their first wedding anniversary."

I was shocked by these revelations. "And those two women are still talking to each other after that?"

"Oh, it didn't last, and both women agreed that Freddie was not worth the trouble," Momma said. "You know what I say. Time heals all wounds, but sometimes, it wounds all heels as well."

"What about Zane Whitlow?" I asked. "It's hard to imagine him raising his voice, let alone killing someone."

"Perhaps now, but that hasn't always been the case. When we were all in school, he had a rather violent temper. I remember him being expelled once for punching another student in the nose for stealing his lunch."

"Zane? Seriously?" Grace asked.

"Not only that, but it was someone he's known for a great many years. The culprit was Hal Embry."

"Zane couldn't *still* be holding a grudge that long for a stolen lunch, could he?" I asked incredulously.

"I don't know. When he was expelled, he lost his scholarship to college and had to go to work for his father in the feed store, a job he detested. That wound could have festered all these years and finally caused him to kill the man."

"I suppose so," I said. "How about Karen Lexington?"

"As a matter of fact, I've known that she was the jealous type ever since I stole her boyfriend," Momma admitted.

"What? She dated my dad? Or was it Phillip?" I asked, baffled by my mother's admission.

"Actually, it was Davey Leadbetter, and we were all in the first grade," Momma admitted. "But that doesn't make her any less aggressive now about anyone who might go after someone she considered her personal property."

"Did she actually *attack* you back then?" I asked.

"No, but she pushed Davey off the monkey bars, and he broke his arm," Momma said. "The thing is, Karen wouldn't apologize. She just said Davey wouldn't have fallen if he hadn't been watching me play hopscotch."

I certainly had a new way of looking at our suspects now.

"I'm having a hard time taking all of this in," I said. When I saw Momma's face cloud up, I quickly added, "It's not that I don't believe you. It just seems so different from who those people have turned out to be now."

"We've all done things in our lives we aren't proud of," Momma said. "Some of us have just had more time to do them."

The dishes were finished, and I drained the soapy water from the sink. As I did, I glanced at the wall clock and saw that it was getting late. "Momma, I hate to eat and run, but Grace and I have to go. We've got an appointment with Zane Whitlow in a few minutes."

"Watch him, Suzanne. Still waters run deep. Would you like me to go with you?"

It had been quite a few years since I'd needed my mommy to protect me, but I appreciated the offer nonetheless. "Thanks, but we'll be careful. Dinner and dessert were both wonderful, but the company was even better."

She smiled and hugged me, and then she did the same for Grace. "Are you *sure* I can't give you both leftovers to take home with you?"

It was tempting, but I knew how much Phillip loved pot roast sandwiches, and if I couldn't have the star of the show, I wasn't interested in any of the walk-on actors. "We're good," I said, and Grace nodded.

"It's just as well. Phillip would have a difficult time forgiving me if there wasn't anything left for him when he came home," Momma said. "Call me when you get home tonight, Suzanne."

"Momma, we're just stopping by to chat with Zane. We're not going to be in danger."

"Call me," she repeated.

"She will," Grace answered for me.

"You too," she admonished my friend.

I thought about pointing out how needless it was for us both to call her since we were going to be together, but I kept the observation to myself. "I love you, Momma."

"And I love you both as well," she said.

Grace and I walked out into the darkness, full and satisfied with both the food and the company we'd just experienced, and braced ourselves to prepare for our meeting with Zane Whitlow. I had to admit that I was a little more leery of it now than I had been before.

It seemed that everyone we suspected had a troubled past.

I just hoped it stayed there and didn't come up to endanger us in the present.

Chapter 10

"I CAN'T BELIEVE HE'S not here," I said a little angrily as we got to Zane Whitlow's house and found his car gone from the driveway. There were no lights on inside the place, not even a porch light left burning for us. "Why are we having so much trouble getting people to talk to us?"

Grace shrugged. "It could just be a coincidence."

"You know how I feel about coincidences," I told her.

"I get it, but can we really live with the alternative, that folks are actively ducking us?" she asked me. "I like that prospect even less."

"So do I," I admitted. "Maybe we've been doing this too long."

"Maybe," Grace agreed, "but are you ready to stop digging into these murders we seem to run across? When do we decide that enough is enough and hang up our magnifying glasses and let someone else take over?"

"Not this time, not with Darby depending on us," I said, "but maybe soon."

"I'll stop when you stop," Grace said as she grinned at me, "but we both know that you've got a highly overinflated sense of justice."

"I resemble that remark," I said with a smirk of my own. "We can't exactly compel folks to talk to us, though. It would be a lot easier if we could flash a badge."

"I'm sure Darby would consider it," Grace said.

"I'm just as certain that you're wrong," I told her. "Besides, that would mean that we'd have to abide by the restraints cops are under during our investigations. Neither one of us wants to see that happen."

"So then we keep the status quo," she answered with a shrug.

"For now, that's all we can do." As I said it, a pair of headlights shifted from the road into the driveway, nearly clipping my Jeep in the process. I jumped back and grabbed Grace's arm at the same time, pulling her out of the vehicle's trajectory.

The car slammed to a halt as Zane got out, his hands shaking. "Are you two all right?"

"You almost hit us!" I shouted.

"My mind was drifting," he admitted, "and I forgot you two were coming by, so I wasn't expecting to see you standing there in my driveway." There was something about the way he said it that made me think that maybe he wasn't that sorry after all.

"Do you mean that seeing my Jeep and then the two of us standing in your driveway didn't shake your memory?" I scolded him.

"It's okay, Suzanne," Grace said as she touched my arm lightly and spoke softly. "We're both fine, and so is your Jeep. Take a deep breath, okay?"

"Why aren't you more upset than I am?" I asked her.

"You saw him before I did. My back was turned to the road, so if you hadn't been paying attention, I would have been a goner."

"I don't know how to apologize to you both," Zane said a bit offhandedly. "Let's not tell anyone this happened, okay? I've had a few incidents lately, and Chief Grant has been hinting that perhaps I should give up driving."

"Is that really that bad an idea?" I asked him, my heart rate finally coming down a bit.

"I might as well be dead if I can't drive," he stated flatly.

"Better you than an innocent bystander," I answered softly.

Thankfully, his hearing was as bad as his driving, because he missed it. "What was that?" he asked me. So, at least he'd heard something.

"She said, 'It's turned out better than it might have,'" Grace lied.

"Yes, that's true. It's the nighttime that gives me the most trouble. If I keep the radio off and don't answer my phone after dark, I should be fine."

"I sincerely hope so," Grace answered.

"I'm afraid I have to go inside now," Zane said shakily, though it still felt artificial to me.

"What about our conversation?" I pushed him.

"I'm so sorry, but it's going to have to wait," he said.

"That's fine with me," Grace said serenely. I suspected she had picked up on the same vibe that I had. "I was hoping to be able to re-assure my husband that you were going to do better behind the wheel, but if you're that shaken by what just happened that you can't even speak with us about Hal Embry's murder, then I'm not at all sure I can do that."

Wow, that was dirty pool, which I applauded. I truly didn't think Zane was all that shaken up by the close call, and I wasn't entirely sure that he hadn't meant to give us a scare with his car when he'd whipped it into the driveway, though he might have come closer to hitting us than he'd intended.

"No, I'm fine now," he said hurriedly, wiping away the vestiges of his tremors. It was clear that he realized that he might have taken his act a little further than he'd meant to. "It just caught me by surprise, that's all."

"Fine. Then let's all go inside and have that chat you promised us earlier."

"Very well," Zane said as he unlocked his front door and let us in.

I didn't see any tremors in his hands as he did so, but I did see him glance back at us with an expression that made me feel uneasy as the porch light came on automatically. He hadn't been ready for my gaze, and it had caught him in a most compromising expression. For some reason, I felt like a fly buzzing straight into a spider's web, and my heart started racing again as the door locked behind us once we were all in-side his lair.

"I'd offer you some tea or coffee, but I won't be up long," Zane said. "Let's just get this over with, shall we?"

"We shall," I said. I didn't even want to sit on the sofa. For some reason, I felt vulnerable there, even with Grace by my side. I had never thought of Zane Whitlow as an imposing man in the past. In fact, I rarely thought of him at all, but Momma's story about his temper had touched a nerve. "Were you backstage when Hal was murdered?"

"Well, that's difficult to say."

"Why is that?" Grace asked.

"We don't know exactly when it happened, do we?" he asked.

"I'm guessing we could narrow the time down to a few minutes," I said. "That's close enough for what we're talking about."

"Hal was being his usual overdramatic self, and it looked as though he wasn't going to even bother showing up. I was ready to go on when he marched in as though he owned the place at the last second. I gave him the prom jacket—we only had one—and I faded back into the wings, watching the other actors prepare," Zane said. "I was off to one side out of the way the entire time. Max doesn't like understudies underfoot," he said with a hint of a wry smile. "In fact, I was even surprised he let us in the wings at all. I'd been watching rehearsals from the audience up to that point, so I was taking it all in."

"Did you look at Hal after he sat down in his chair?" I asked him softly.

"I might have glanced his way a few times," Zane admitted. "Mostly, I was wondering how it would feel going on. I've got to admit, I didn't envy him. I've just had a few small roles in the past, never one so challenging."

"Did anything unusual happen before the play started?" Grace asked him.

"What do you mean?"

"Well, were there any arguments, any distractions, things like that?" I prodded.

"You heard about that, did you?" Zane asked warily.

"We did," I said. "What was it all about?"

In a calm and measured voice, Zane said, "I told him he didn't deserve the part, that he was disrespecting everyone there by showing up late. I said that if he wasn't going to take it seriously, maybe he shouldn't bother showing up at all."

"What did he say to that?" Grace asked him.

"He told me that I wasn't fit to play the role of the janitor," Zane said angrily.

"I take it it's a small role?" I asked gently.

"The part has no lines at all. He just sweeps up once during the third act," Zane answered icily.

"Where did you go after that? We heard that you stormed offstage," I pointed out.

"I cooled off in an instant, then I crept back into the shadows offstage where no one could see me. There was no way I was going to let him ruin the experience for me. Things were pretty crazy as everyone prepared, and Hal wouldn't leave his chair when Max drew the rest of the cast together. Your ex wasn't happy about it, but he let it slide. Hal believed himself to be a method actor, so we weren't allowed to speak with him before the curtain went up. I violated some unwritten rule by daring to challenge him, and I didn't want to catch Max's eye. He might have evicted me from backstage just to placate Hal's ego."

"So you were off to one side while Hal was sitting alone?" I asked. If we could find someone to alibi him, we could cross Zane off our list.

"I was," Zane explained. "Max said a few words, gave everyone kind of a pep talk, and then he had the lights turned off for ten seconds of silence before things were to begin."

"He did *what*? Why am I just hearing about this now?" I asked him. It explained a great deal as to how someone had managed to kill Hal Embry on a crowded stage before a performance without anyone else seeing the murder.

"It's something Max said he'd always wanted to do," Zane said. "Clearly you've never been in one of his productions. He was always trying one thing or another to get his players focused on the performance at hand."

"He tried to recruit me a time or two when we were married," I admitted, "but I hated the idea of being so exposed on stage in front of all of those people."

"I can understand that feeling," Zane said.

"Did you hear anything unusual during the ten seconds of darkness?" Grace asked him.

"There was some scuffling of feet, a cough or two—enough of a distraction that Max reminded us that silence was important—but I didn't hear Hal cry out, if that's what you're asking. Why didn't he make a noise if that was when he was stabbed?"

"Maybe the killer used one hand on the knife, and the other went over Hal's mouth," I wondered out loud, struck by how grisly that image was.

"I suppose that's possible," Zane said.

"You didn't all hold hands or anything, did you?" Grace asked him.

"No, we weren't singing vespers at summer camp," Zane explained icily. "It's supposed to be a moment for everyone to focus on what was to come."

"So then *anyone* could have stabbed him," I said, disappointed that my first husband had inadvertently helped the killer strike.

"I don't know about that. All I can say for sure is that it wasn't me," Zane said.

"As much as we'd like to believe you, we can't just take your word for it," I told him gently.

"I told you! I was in the wings on the other side of the stage," Zane said, a bit heated. "I *couldn't* have made it across to Hal, stabbed him, and then made it back in that short amount of time."

"Can anyone else confirm that?" I asked.

"Are you calling me a liar, Suzanne?" Zane said as he took a step toward me. Wow. I'd always thought of him as a meek kind of guy, but he didn't seem that way to me at the moment.

I took a step back. "Of course not, but you have to understand that we just can't take your word for it."

"I don't see why not, because it is the complete unvarnished truth. I'm finished with you both. You need to leave now," he said brusquely as he moved toward his front door.

Grace tried to mollify him. "Zane, we *have* to ask tough questions. Surely *someone* saw you there. Perhaps Hillary Teal?"

"I didn't see her, or anyone else for that matter," he explained. "Besides, nobody notices an *understudy*."

He sounded quite resentful about the fact. I thought about leaving quietly, but he was already upset with us, so I decided to push him just a bit more to see how he'd react.

"One last thing," I said as Grace and I reached the door. "How did you feel about Hal Embry? The truth."

"It's no secret that I didn't care for him, but that doesn't mean that I wanted him dead," he snapped at us as Grace and I stepped out onto the porch.

"We hear you had a grudge against him that dated back to high school," I pushed.

His face went white at the comment, and I expected him to explode. Instead, he did something that alarmed me even more. He stared at me with dead eyes, and then he gently closed the door on us.

"Let's get out of here," Grace said as she grabbed my arm. "That guy was really creeping me out."

"I know," I told her as we hurried to my Jeep. "I used to think he was just this quiet, nondescript guy, but after what Momma told us and with what we just saw, I'm a little scared of the man right now."

"Just a little?" Grace asked. "You're a braver woman than I am if it's just a little. That bit at the end was chilling."

"I agree, but if we can find someone who can swear he didn't have time to kill Hal, we might have to mark him off our list of suspects," I said.

"That's true enough, but in the meantime, he's staying right at the top," Grace answered as we headed back to our respective homes.

"Even above the three tarts?" I asked her.

"Let's just say that at the moment, *everyone's* tied for the top spot," Grace said. "I don't know about you, but I'm going to deadbolt my door tonight."

"You don't seriously think he'd come after us, do you?" I asked her.

"I don't know, and that's what scares me so much. Even if it turns out that he didn't do it, I'm never going to look at that man the same way again."

I pulled into her driveway and shut off the engine. "That's the problem with finding out too much about people or really getting to know them. Sometimes you learn more than you want to about them."

"It's definitely a bad part of our investigations," Grace agreed. "Want to come in for some coffee? What am I saying? It's past your bedtime, isn't it?"

I answered with a yawn. "A little bit, but I can stay a minute or two."

She put a hand on my arm. "I'll be fine. Go home. Go to bed. But don't forget to deadbolt the front door."

"Yes, Momma," I said, something that triggered a promise we'd made earlier. "Let's get this out of the way all at once, shall we?"

She nodded, and I pulled out my phone and called Momma. "Hey, we're back home," I told her when she picked up.

"Grace as well?"

"I'm right here, Dot," she chimed in.

"Are you two spending the night together?" my mother asked us.

"No. I'm dropping Grace off at her place, and then I'm heading home," I admitted.

"Grace, thank you for calling. Suzanne, I'll speak with you in four minutes."

"Seriously? You're going to time me?" I asked her incredulously.

"That should give you ample time to drive home, park, go inside, and lock the door behind you. If I haven't heard from you in six minutes, I'm calling the police."

"Wow, I get a whole two minutes of leeway?" I asked her.

"Tick, tick, tick," Momma said, and then she hung up.

I shook my head and put my phone away. "It's official. My mother has lost her mind."

"She's just worried about you, Suzanne."

"She's worried about both of us," I reminded her, "but you'd better get out so I can meet my impromptu curfew. See you tomorrow?"

"You bet," she said. "I'm sorry about your double shift of donut making."

"It'll be fine," I told her. "Now go. Momma wasn't joking. If I don't make it in time, I'm going to have Darby Jones showing up on my doorstep two minutes later."

I made it, though just barely. Thirty seconds before my extended deadline was set to expire, I dialed Momma's number. "Stop the clock," I said.

"Are you safely at home?"

"I am," I admitted.

"Behind locked doors?"

"Yes, ma'am."

"Good. I apologize if I worry too much, but you're the only child I have."

"Hey, it's not my fault you and Dad didn't have any spares," I said. "Why were you so worried about us, anyway?"

She paused a moment before she answered. "I *always* worry about you, Suzanne, and when you're investigating a murder, it's even worse.

There's a killer out there among us, and I don't want them coming after you. How was your interview with Zane Whitlow?"

"It didn't go great," I said, and then I told her about what had happened. "Should we be worried about him, Momma?"

"Well, I wouldn't turn my back on him until this is over, but I wouldn't be too concerned. He usually does a good job keeping his temper in check. You must have hit a nerve tonight when you questioned him."

"Is that a good thing or a bad one?" I asked.

"Find the killer, and then you'll know," she answered. "Good night, Suzanne. I love you."

"I love you too, Momma," I said, and then I ended the call. I'd been a little miffed that she'd put me on a deadline to make it home so quickly, but she'd done it out of love, so I couldn't be all that upset with her.

I decided to take a quick shower before bed. It felt much better washing away the afternoon's many failures, but I regretted it the moment I checked my phone before crawling into bed.

Jake had called, and I'd missed it.

"Hey, Suzanne,

We came into town for a bite, so I thought I'd give you a call. You must already be asleep. I hope everything's going well there. It's nice to get away, but I miss you. Is that corny? I can't be away from you for very long at all until I find myself pining away. Some tough ex-cop, huh? Anyway, just wanted to say good night and tell you that I love you. That's it. Bye."

It was sweet, and I'd cherish that voicemail for a long time to come, but I would have much rather spoken to him on the phone or, better yet, in person.

I chalked it up to just another failure in a long line of them. Things hadn't gone my way so far, but like the lady said, tomorrow was another day.

I just hoped that we managed to narrow things down a bit. It was too much to expect to find the killer tomorrow, but at the very least, I wanted to get our list down to a more manageable number. As things stood, we had an entire cast and crew of the play to look at, and with Max's ten-second blackout, it was going to be even harder than I'd thought.

Chapter 11

MY MORNING DID NOT start off any better than my night before had. I had no hot water for my shower, something that was an absolute requirement for me. My idea of roughing it was when I ran out of chocolate, so I wasn't happy taking an icy, if abbreviated, shower. I'd have to call someone to fix it. There was no way that I was going to willingly take another cold shower.

I was surprised to see Emma's car parked in her usual spot when I got to Donut Hearts. The lights were already on in the kitchen. "Hello? Emma? Is that you?"

"Who else would it be?" she asked as she came out from the back.

"I don't know, a robber?" I asked.

"Seriously? What would they take?" she asked with a hint of laughter in her voice. "Flour? Sugar? I know our prices have been going up lately, but I don't think we have to worry about anyone trying to steal supplies from us."

"What are you doing here?" I asked as I poured myself a cup of coffee. It was nice not having to wait for it, as was my usual custom, and the hot liquid took off some of the chill I'd experienced with my shower.

"Grace called me last night," she said.

"Okay," I answered, waiting for the rest of the story.

"She told me about volunteering you to make extra donuts for the wake, so she asked me to stay later and lend you a hand."

"She shouldn't have asked, and you don't have to do it," I said quickly. "Wait a second. If you're offering to help me *after* work, why are you here now?" It was maybe just a bit early for mind games for me. I mostly made donuts on autopilot until I woke up fully, though the icy shower had managed to knock a few cobwebs out of my mind.

"I had a better idea. We can double up batches this morning if we work through our break time, and you can get out at your regular time," she explained with a grin. "What do you say? It will be fun."

I took a sip of coffee before I answered. "So what you're telling me is that you can't help me this afternoon, but you were willing to come in early to help me knock them out first thing."

"I prefer to think of it as managing our available time and resources to better use," she said.

"Did you get that from one of your business classes?" I asked her with a slight smile. Her enthusiasm was infectious.

"Econ 302," she said. "So, what do you say?"

"I believe there's only one thing left for me to say," I told her. "Thank you."

"Let's make donuts!" she said, as if she were on a game show and not standing in Donut Hearts in the middle of the night.

We finished up both double batches at twenty till six, which was when we usually opened the doors for our customers. "How did that happen?" I asked her in wonder as she finished up another load of dishes.

"We didn't take our break, remember?" she asked. "Plus, how much more trouble is it to make twice as much when you break it down logically?"

I looked around at the largesse around us. "I think we went a little overboard. I don't need this many donuts for the day, or for the wake."

"Well, since we've already made them, I *could* take some off your hands," she said a bit shyly.

"What are you going to do with ten dozen donuts?" I asked.

"I'd love to take them all to the bake sale they're having at the grade school today," Emma admitted.

I had to laugh. "That was your plan all along, wasn't it?"

"I was going to come in and ask your permission anyway, but when Grace called me last night, I thought it sounded perfect. You're not angry, are you?"

"No, of course not," I said as I hugged her. "I'll even cover the supplies we used."

"Not necessary. Grace is handling the financial end of it," Emma said.

"Let me get this straight. You conned me into helping you make donuts for the school bake sale and then got Grace to foot the bill?"

"That sounds bad when you say it like that," she admitted.

"Are you kidding? I think this business degree you're getting is amazing. I'm impressed. What did you have to promise for Grace to sponsor it?"

"What makes you think there's a catch?" she asked me.

I smiled at her. "You might be good, but Grace is better. Don't let it bother you. She's a lot slicker than I am too."

"We're putting a sign up at the table that it's being sponsored by Donut Hearts and her cosmetics company. I've got a basket of free samples for the parents working the booths, and I promised her some kind of promotion at Barton's restaurant when we open."

"That sounds fair to me," I said, suppressing my smile. Leave it to Grace to make everyone come out a winner. I had my donuts for the day and for the wake, Emma was able to help out at the school bake sale, and Grace got all of the PR she needed to justify it on her expense account.

"If you don't mind, I'd like to run these over to the school before we open," Emma said.

"That's fine with me. Do you need a hand?"

"No, I've got one of the dads coming by with his truck," she answered.

"What's Barton going to think about that?" I asked her with a smile.

"He's not even going to notice. My fiancé only has eyes for Twenty-First Southern these days," she answered.

The dad, somewhere in his thirties, knocked on the front door and grinned at Emma. "Is there a Mrs. Volunteer?" I asked Emma softly. "He's smiling at you as though you invented Christmas."

"He's divorced," my assistant said, blushing a little as she said it.

"He's a good-looking man," I told her.

"Suzanne, you're a married woman."

"You're not. Be careful that you don't lead him on. I'd hate for you to break his heart."

"Yes, Mom," she said with a frown.

"You couldn't pay me a better compliment," I said as I unlocked the door. "Hi, I'm Suzanne Hart. We haven't met, have we?"

"No, ma'am, but I'm new in town. My name is Jason Will. We really appreciate you donating your donuts."

"All the credit for that goes to Emma, Jason," I said with a smile.

"I think it's safe if we spread it around a bit," he answered, smiling.

Once I got everything loaded up on carts to take to his truck, I was surprised to see someone else approaching the shop.

It wasn't the fact that she was carrying a gift bag that caught me off guard though.

It was Geneva Swift, my mother's assistant.

"I'm sorry, Geneva, but we're not open yet," I told her as she approached.

"I'm not here for the donuts, as wonderful as they smell," she said pleasantly. "Suzanne, can I have a moment of your time?"

There really wasn't anything else for me to do but wait until opening time, but Geneva and I hadn't exactly gotten along since my mother had hired her as her assistant. Still, if I turned her away without a good reason, Momma wouldn't be pleased about it. "Come on in."

She stepped inside, and I locked the door behind her.

"What's up?" I asked.

Geneva thrust the gift bag in her hands out to me. "This is for you."

"Seriously? It's not my birthday," I said as I took it a little reluctantly. "What's the occasion?"

"It's an apology," Geneva said contritely. "I know we haven't gotten along, and I want you to know that it's my fault entirely. I'd like a fresh start."

"That's totally unnecessary," I said a little uncomfortably.

"I don't agree. Suzanne, your mother speaks so highly of you that I've been intimidated by you since the moment we first met. I know I can never live up to your standards. It's obvious you were your mother's first choice for her assistant and not me, and I had a tough time dealing with it."

I couldn't be bought with idle flattery, but it appeared that I could be rented, especially when the apology seemed so genuine. "Momma loves working with you," I told her, which was true enough.

"I do my best, but I've decided that it's a foolish task trying to outdo you. The most I can do is the best I can do, you know? I'd really like us to be friends, if you can see it in your heart to forgive me. I often make a terrible first impression, but I'm getting better at second ones. What do you say?"

The desire in her expression for a fresh start was so obvious that I had no real choice but to accept it.

I looked at her steadily for a few moments before I answered, "I suppose that depends."

"On what?"

"On what you brought me," I said with a smile.

She grinned. "I hope you like them."

"There's only one way to find out." I opened the bag and pulled out the first gift, a lovely pair of stud earrings sporting tiny chocolate donuts. "How sweet."

"Do you like them?" she asked eagerly. "I asked around to see if you had any hobbies, but no one seemed to be able to come up with any. It appears your life revolves around donuts, so I decided to focus on that."

"What can I say?" I answered with a grin. "I'm a woman of limited interests. It's true enough. I happen to love donuts, so you're in luck."

In short order I pulled out drink coasters, Christmas ornaments, and even pencil erasers, all in the shape of donuts and decorated as such.

"Is it too much?" she asked.

"I'd say it's just right," I told her as I took off my own earrings and replaced them with the donut studs she'd just given me. "How do they look?"

"Like they belong on your earlobes," she said with a smile.

"Thank you, Geneva. If I'm being honest, I've been a little resentful of you too. Momma seems to think the world of you," I told her frankly.

"I do my best, but the sun rises and sets by you, at least according to her," Geneva replied.

"Let's just admit that we're both spectacular and leave it at that, then," I told her with a grin.

She smiled back brightly at me. "I'm good with that if you are. Thank you, Suzanne."

"I'm the one who should be thanking you," I said as I held up my bag of goodies. "After all, I got presents. At least let me buy you a donut before you go." That was the true test. If we were going to coexist on this planet, she needed to eat one of my donuts, whether she wanted to or not. Geneva had turned my offer down on more than one occasion in the past, but I could tell that she sensed this was a deal breaker.

"I'd love one of those strawberry iced ones," she said as she pointed to the case.

"You've got it. In fact, I'll join you," I said as I plated up two donuts. After all, it would have been rude not to do it, and I loved donuts just as much as the next gal.

If not more, truth be told.

I saw her reach her hand into her purse out of the corner of my eye, and without looking directly at her, I said, "If you're reaching for your wallet, we're going to have a problem."

I wasn't sure if that was what she'd been doing, but if it was, she quickly changed direction. "I was just making sure that my phone was turned on. I would never dream of offering to pay you for something that was clearly meant as a goodwill gesture."

"Maybe we have a chance of getting along after all," I said with a smile. "That was smooth."

"Hey, I'm not just a pretty face," she answered with a grin of her own.

I poured us two coffees, and she carried our plates to the nicest sofa in the eating area, a diagonally placed spot that showed off the park across the street.

I wouldn't say that we were best friends by the time we finished, but we'd certainly worked out a new relationship. Once I started to get to know her, I actually found myself liking her.

Geneva was gone by the time Emma came back. My assistant spotted the empty mugs and plates and asked, "Did you have company while I was gone?"

"Hey, I have the right to see other people too," I told her mockingly.

"True," she said, and then she spotted the bag Geneva had brought me. "Suzanne, you shouldn't have."

As she reached for the bag, I said, "Good, because I didn't. That's mine."

Emma's eyebrows rose. "Does Jake know someone's bringing you presents?"

"He won't mind," I told her. "Momma's assistant came by, and we buried the hatchet."

Emma looked around. "That's funny, I don't see any blood."

"It was nice, actually," I admitted.

Emma glanced at me and then took a second look at my earlobes. "Those are new."

"Cool, aren't they?" I asked.

"Very."

"How did the donation go?" I asked her, not really wanting to talk about my conversation with Geneva.

"The donuts were a massive hit," she said as I cleaned off the plates and mugs. "You've got some real fans at that school."

"Why me? You're the one who made it happen. Well, you and Grace."

"What can I say? The kids just love the Donut Lady. You don't mind if they call you that, do you?"

"To my face or behind my back?" I asked with a smile. "It doesn't matter. Strike that question. Honestly, I've been called a lot worse. I'll take it." I glanced at the clock and saw that it was time to open. "Are you ready to face the crowd out there dying to get in?"

Emma looked outside at an empty sidewalk in front of the shop. "I think we can handle it between the two of us," she said.

At that moment, my mother—never known for being such an early visitor to my shop—drove up and parked in front of Donut Hearts.

From the expression on her face, I could easily tell that she wasn't pleased about something, and I had a feeling that I was about to learn all about it.

Chapter 12

"GOOD MORNING," I TOLD her cheerfully, hoping that her visit was nothing that was going to be too upsetting to either one of us.

"Suzanne, we need to talk," she said solemnly.

"That's never a good sign, is it?" I asked her. "May I get you some coffee and a donut first?"

"I'm sorry, but I didn't come here for your treats, as delightful as they are," she said. "I need to warn you about something."

"What have you heard? Is someone coming after me? Is it Zane?" I asked her. Sadly, it wouldn't be the first time someone had been angered to the point of violence due to one of my investigations. In the course of my amateur sleuthing, I'd made more than my fair share of enemies in April Springs and the surrounding towns.

"Of course not. At least not that I'm aware of. Geneva asked for some time off this morning so she could speak with you."

"What time does she report for work, Momma? She's already come and gone."

"I was afraid of that. Why can't you two work things out? You're both bright, accomplished young women."

"We did," I said, but it clearly didn't register with my mother.

"I mean really, I would have thought that you'd.... Hold on. What did you just say?"

"She came by with some peace offerings, then we had donuts and coffee and worked things out. Well, we made a good start at it, anyway. She bought me these earrings. Aren't they sweet?"

"Very," Momma said. "Is that all it took?"

"Like I said, we had some donuts and a chat too. We understand each other a bit better now than we did before. You're right. I can see why you hired her and why you like her."

"I'm so glad," Momma said. She glanced at the display case. "Is there any way I can have half a lemon-filled donut?"

"I'm sorry, but we don't sell them that way," I told her with a grin.

"I can't eat an entire one alone," Momma said ruefully. "Oh, well."

"How about if we split one?" I asked her. I'd already had a donut with Geneva, but there was no way I wasn't going to split one with my mother too. "I'll just grab a knife."

"If it's not too much trouble," she said.

"Not at all," I answered as I grabbed one of the donuts in question and cut it in two. I knew enough that if I made one section smaller than the other, then *that* would be the one Momma would choose. I made one slightly smaller, but I made sure that it was the end that had the hole where I'd filled the donut. I liked to pack my filled donuts, so I knew that piece would have more filling than the other one. I laid the two plates side by side on the counter. "You choose," I said.

As I'd predicted, she chose the smaller, though more stuffed, piece.

"What are you smiling about, Suzanne?"

I'd have to be more careful with my open displays of pleasure around her, especially when I was trying to do something nice for her. "I'm just happy to see you," I said, which was the truth, though certainly not all of it.

"I feel the very same way," she answered. "This is delightful," she added after she took a bite. "How do you manage to pack so much filling into these?"

I wasn't about to admit what I'd done. "What can I say? Practice makes perfect. Is that the only reason you came by, to warn me about Geneva?"

"Well, seeing you as well is an obvious bonus," she answered. "How are things otherwise with you?"

"Besides a cold shower this morning, I can't complain."

She frowned. "Why on earth are you taking cold showers? It's not some new kind of health trend, is it?"

"How would I know?" I asked her with a grin. "I'm not exactly up on that kind of thing. No, my hot water heater must have died sometime last night, because this morning, it wasn't working."

"Suzanne, it's a water heater, not a hot water heater. If the water were already hot, why would it need to be heated again?" I could always count on my mother to point out the obvious.

"Call it what you'd like, but it's not even doing that now."

She pulled out her phone. Who in the world was she calling at six in the morning? She'd never answered how early Geneva had to get to work, and I wasn't going to ask. There were some things I would rather not know, especially since I'd been tempted to take that job myself once upon a time. "Cynthia? Dot. I need you to go by my daughter's cottage and look at her water heater." She said the last bit looking at me as if to reaffirm that she'd said it properly and not me. "Yes, replace it if it's necessary and put it on my account. The key is under the third rock by the front door and just beneath the porch. Thank you."

"Momma, you didn't have to do that," I said after she hung up. "Surely your plumber has better things to do than to take care of me."

"I can always cancel the work order if you'd prefer," she said as she pulled her phone out again.

It didn't take me more than a split second to realize that would be a very bad idea. "I'm sorry, what I meant to say was thank you very much for looking out for me. I appreciate it."

Momma smiled brightly and patted my cheek affectionately. "Of course. She was going to be working for me on one of my rentals today anyway, so why not take advantage of the situation? Cynthia will have you right as rain in no time. She's quite good."

"So I've heard. I love that you have a female plumber," I told her.

"Her sex has nothing to do with it, Suzanne," Momma told me. "She's the most qualified plumber I know since her father retired. That's why I use her."

"But it doesn't hurt that she's a woman too, does it?" I asked her.

"Of course not," Momma admitted.

"That's all I'm saying."

"What is that, exactly?"

"Never mind," I said. "If I need a new h...water heater, I'd be glad to pay for it myself."

"Nonsense. Consider it my gift to you and your husband. Did Jake call you last night as well? Phillip touched base, and he is having the time of his life."

I didn't really need that reminder. "As a matter of fact, I was in the shower when Jake called. By the time I got out, he was out of range again."

"I'm sorry, but the boys are having a lovely time," Momma replied.

"Please call Jake a boy in front of me the next time you see him," I told her.

"He won't mind, coming from me," she said.

"Of course he won't," I answered, knowing that it was true. "Anyway, thanks for handling my issue with the heater."

"I couldn't be more delighted to be able to do it, my dear child," Momma answered. "Now I must be off," she said as she pushed her plate away. She'd managed to eat a third of the half donut I'd given her, but I wasn't about to say anything about it. Momma stayed neat and trim by limiting her portions. I couldn't abandon part of a donut on my plate any more than I could step over a hundred-dollar bill without bending over and picking it up.

"Have a great day, Momma," I said.

I waited until she was gone. My half had been eaten quickly. I waited until the count of five, and then I gobbled down her remnant as well. My waistline might not thank me, but my conscience certainly would.

After all, no donut deserves to go partially consumed, at least in this case.

"Celia, what brings you by the shop?" I asked one of the three tarts as she came in a few hours later.

"I wanted to be certain that you were still providing the refreshments for the wake later this afternoon," she said. "I understand it's short notice, but we greatly appreciate the gesture."

"As a matter of fact, they're already finished and boxed in back," I said. To lay it on, I added, "Emma and I both had to work through our break, but we understand how important it is to say goodbye to Hal properly."

In response, she dabbed at a tear in the corner of her eye, or more accurately, where one would have been if she'd actually been crying.

She hadn't.

Leave it to an actress, amateur or professional, to act when the opportunity arose. I'd learned that early on in my marriage to Max, so I knew the signs to watch for.

"You're so understanding," she said, even making her voice choke up a bit as she said the last part.

"I'm curious about something," I said, "now that I have you here."

"Suzanne, I've already apologized for leaving the house without phoning you, but Geraldine was insistent, and I really didn't feel as though I could say no to her."

"Why exactly did she need to see you so urgently?" I asked her. "Also, you were about to tell us something in front of her house, but she stopped you. What was that all about?" I figured Celia had come to Donut Hearts willingly, so if I decided to push her a bit about her behavior the day before, I was well within my rights. It wasn't as though I was going after a steady customer, anyway.

Celia looked around my empty shop, and then she glanced toward the back. "Don't worry," I told her. "Emma is doing dishes, and she plays such loud music on her earbuds that I don't know how she can hear herself think, let alone eavesdrop on our conversation."

Celia cocked an ear, straining to hear her music, and I realized that we were in dead silence. "Like I said, she has those earbud thingies in. That's why it's so quiet," I explained.

"Yes, I'm familiar with the concept, but how do you know she's not listening to us instead?"

"Emma, we're being robbed! Help!" I shouted.

There was no response from the kitchen, and I opened the door so Celia could see that my assistant was buried up to her elbows in soapsuds. "See?" I pointed out as I let the door close, all without Emma being the wiser.

"Geraldine did tell me something rather unsettling," Celia said as her brow furrowed. "I haven't quite known what to do with the information, to be honest with you."

"You'll feel better if you tell someone else," I reassured her. "I've been told that I'm a good listener. What did she say, Celia?"

She was about to tell me when George Morris, our mayor and usually someone extremely welcome in Donut Hearts, came in, accompanied by Officer Rick Handler of the April Springs Police Department. "I'm telling you, Rick, Mrs. Perkins claims there's a bear in her backyard."

"Mr. Mayor, Kate Baylor's dogs bark at shadows on that back porch of hers, and she swears it's either an armed intruder, Bigfoot, or a bear."

"Monet and Degas are a pair of rowdy pups," George admitted when he noticed Celia was standing there with me. "Good morning, ladies," he said.

Celia barely made eye contact with either man as she rushed for the door.

"Celia, I'm here for you," I called out.

She ignored the offer. "Thank you again for your donation, Suzanne. I'll see you later."

George looked after her once she was gone. "Was it something I said?"

"I can't imagine any eligible woman in town running away from you, Mr. Mayor," Rick said with a laugh.

"Then it must have been you. Anyway, go over and see if you can calm Mrs. Baylor down, would you?" He frowned a moment and then added, "Strike that. Tell your acting chief, and then ask him what you should do. I keep breaking the chain of command. I've really got to stop doing that."

"You're not breaking anything," Officer Handler said glumly. "Darby, I mean Acting Chief of Police Jones, said the same thing."

"Then why are you still here?" George asked him, the levity gone from his voice. "You were given instructions. I suggest you follow them, Officer."

The change of intonation wasn't lost on Officer Handler. "Yes, sir. I'm on it."

He gave one loving look back at my display cases, and then he was gone.

"I can't wait for Stephen Grant to get back from vacation," George said. "There aren't any discipline problems when he's around."

"It's probably hard on everyone," I said. "Give Rick a break."

"I appreciate the advice, and I'll certainly take it under consideration," the mayor said by rote.

"In other words, stay out of official police business and stick to my own knitting," I told him with a slight grin.

"That sounds like something your mother would say," he told me.

"You are correct, sir," I answered. "I like to say 'sorry for the inconvenience' when one of my customers complains about something I'm doing."

"It's the same principle, isn't it?" George asked. "What was going on with Celia Laslow?"

"Do you know her well?" I asked.

The mayor mumbled something under his breath that I couldn't quite catch.

"Excuse me, Mr. Mayor?"

"I said we might have gone out a time or two a few years ago," he admitted. "Blast it all, is that why she bolted out of here? It was over a long time ago. I hadn't realized that I'd meant that much to her."

"You need to take your ego down a peg, George. That had *nothing* to do with you," I told him.

"Rick Handler? You're kidding."

"Not because of what you're thinking," I told him. "I suspect it was because he was in uniform."

"Is she worried she might say something she shouldn't about Hal Embry's murder?" the mayor asked me.

"Before you came in, she was about to share something juicy with me that Geraldine Morgan told her yesterday," I admitted.

"And I managed to mess that up for you by walking in Donut Hearts with a cop, no less. Sorry about that."

"No worries," I said, though I wasn't entirely pleased that Celia had bolted before talking to me.

"Why was she thanking you for your donation? She didn't have anything to do with the school bake sale, did she?"

"How did you know about that?" I asked him.

"I'm the mayor. I know everything," George said smugly.

I started laughing, and after a second, he joined me. "I know it sounds insane, but some people actually believe that. So, what else are you contributing to?"

"There's going to be a wake for Hal Embry at the auditorium this afternoon," I admitted. "The three...lead actresses are hosting it. I'd invite you, but it's cast and crew only."

"And donut makers as well, I'm assuming," he said.

"Well, if I linger a bit after delivering so many treats, surely no one will be able to object," I said coyly.

"And if they do, I'm certain you'll find a way to stay, anyway," George said with a smile. "How goes the investigation?"

"I'd tell you all about it, but it would only take ten seconds, so I'm not sure what we'd do with the rest of our time," I said.

"Is it really as bad as all that?" he asked me.

"Just about. Would you like an old-fashioned donut and a cup of coffee?" I asked him, since that was his most recent regular order.

"No, I'm going to shake things up today," he said with a soft smile.

"*Two* old-fashioned donuts and a coffee to go?" I guessed.

He frowned. "Blast it, Suzanne, remind me never to play poker with you. You're too good at reading me."

"We've known each other a very long time, Mr. Mayor," I reminded him.

"Longer than either one of us would care to admit, most likely," he answered as he took bag and cup with him after paying me. I didn't bother offering him the goodies on the house. I just took his money and then handed him his change.

"Happy hunting," George said as he paused at the door.

"Thanks. We need it," I answered.

"I'm putting my money on you and Grace," he answered with a grin.

"Us, and not your depleted police force?" I asked him.

"I believe it's going to be a lovely day," the mayor said, and then he nodded in my direction as he left. George Morris hadn't been born into his role as our mayor of April Springs. In fact, he'd been mostly tricked into the job, but it turned out that he was very good at it, and every day he spent in office, he got better and better. Momma had rigged the entire thing from the beginning, and she'd been right.

It made me wonder why I'd ever doubted her, but I wasn't about to tell her that.

Her ego was healthy enough without me piling praise on too.

Chapter 13

"SO, I UNDERSTAND THEY got you too," Max said as he walked into Donut Hearts a little after ten that morning. "I'm hosting a wake I didn't want to even be a part of, and you're catering it."

"I have an ulterior motive," I told him. "What's your excuse?"

"I'm doing it mostly to get the three tarts off my back," he admitted. "Have you had any luck with your investigation?"

"Not much so far, but I have high hopes for this afternoon. Can I get you something?"

He looked at the display cases and pointed to a cinnamon twist. "Those look good. Do you have any stuffed with apple inside them?"

"Do you mean like a fritter?" I asked him.

"More like a small pie, with a cinnamon coating too," he suggested.

"Tell you what. I'll whip one up just for you if you let me direct your next play," I answered with a smile. "I mean since we're trading jobs and all."

"Okay, take it easy. I was just asking," he responded, holding up his palms in a gesture of peace.

"Sorry, I may have overreacted," I said. There were a few customers eating their donuts in peace, but nobody needed me at the moment. "Stay right there. I'll be back."

"I didn't mean to run you off," he interjected.

"Just don't leave," I told him as I grabbed a cinnamon twist and headed in back.

Emma looked up from her dishes. "Taking a snack break?" she asked me with a grin.

"I'm doing something for Max," I said as I got some apple filling and laced a line of it across the twist and then added an extra dash of cinnamon sugar. It looked pretty good, so I plated it and took it out to Max. "There you go," I told him.

"That looks great. What do I owe you?"

"Take a bite and tell me what you think," I countered.

He shrugged. "That's an offer too good to refuse." He took a bite, pretended to think about it, and then polished it off in two more quick tastes. "I'm still not sure. Maybe I should try another one before I give you my opinion."

I laughed. "I think I just got it."

"It was amazing," he admitted.

"Good to know," I answered, filing it away in my mind for a later offering. I was constantly trying to shake things up at Donut Hearts, so a new addition would be welcome, especially come autumn when apples were in season.

Max lowered his voice. "If you've got the time, I may be able to give you more insights into any of your suspects that are involved in the play."

"You're kidding, right? They *all* are," I told him.

Max looked around. "Any chance you could get Emma to take over the front for a bit? We could go over to the park where no one would be able to overhear us."

"Since when were you that worried about your reputation?" I asked my ex.

"If my actors find out that I've been telling tales about them behind their backs, I might have trouble getting any of them to sign on for my next production."

"That makes sense," I said as I stuck my head in through the kitchen door. "Cover the front for me for a few?" I asked Emma.

"Sure. Are you going to take that break we missed this morning?"

"Max wants to talk to me about something, in private," I told her, not mentioning that it was about Hal Embry's murder.

"Oh, that can't be good," she said.

"I wouldn't think so, no," I told her.

"Take your time. My fingers are getting a little pruney anyway. I feel as though I've been doing dishes all day."

"Maybe that's because you have," I said with a grin. "Thanks."

I took my apron off and hung it up.

"Let's go," I told him after I walked out of the kitchen, and he followed me out the door, looking back at the shop as he did so when I glanced in his direction.

"Was there something else you needed?" I asked.

"Another donut would be nice," he admitted.

"Ask me again after we chat."

Max frowned. "Fine. Who all is still on your list?"

I didn't start talking until we were alone on a bench in the park diagonally across from the donut shop and close to the cottage I shared with my second, and much better, husband. "Besides Celia, Geraldine, and Vivian, we're looking at Zane, Hillary, and Karen," I told him.

Max looked shocked. "You're kidding, right?"

"Do I look as though I'm kidding?" I asked him. "Why? Is there some reason to take any of them off of it?"

"Well, Karen wasn't due to go on until the second act. She's got a bit part, and she resented it, so she always made it a point not to show up until later."

That was when it hit me. Karen had told us that she'd been working on her costume, but she hadn't admitted that she'd missed the murder itself. Why hadn't she mentioned that? It would have been the first thing I would have said if I'd been in her shoes. "Did you see her backstage at all?"

"No, and I notice *everyone* who's there," Max answered. "Well, usually, but things were a bit crazy at the time, so I could be wrong about that."

"Is there *any* chance she could have snuck on and back off while you were doing your ten seconds of darkness?" I asked him. "By the way, I could have really used that information earlier. Didn't you think it was pertinent to my investigation?"

"I'm so sorry about that," Max replied sheepishly. "So much had happened that it didn't occur to me until later, and by this morning, I'd forgotten to tell you about it."

"What else are you failing to mention?" I asked him. "Is there anything *else* that you've forgotten to tell me?"

"Suzanne, if I've forgotten it, how would I know?"

"That's a fair point," I said. "Do me a favor. Ask around later and see if anyone else saw Karen there before the murder."

"I can do better than that," he said. "Let me make a few calls." He stepped away, and as he spoke softly into the phone, I looked around at the lovely day we were having. It wasn't too hot yet, but I knew those days were coming soon. We didn't live in the South for nothing, after all. I never really minded the heat; it was the humidity that always seemed to get to me.

Max put his phone away. "Karen Lexington is in the clear."

"How can you be so sure?" I asked him.

"We have a student interning with us in the costume department, and she was with Karen during the murder, helping her cinch up a waistline that I thought was already as tight as it could get."

I should have been happy taking her name off my list, but I'd favored her as a lead suspect, so it was a little disheartening to know that she hadn't done it.

"Is there anybody else you can eliminate?"

"I'm curious about something. Why are you looking at Hillary and Zane? I understand the three tarts, and honestly, any one of them could have done it out of sheer spite, but why those two?"

"Zane had a history of conflict with Hal that went back to high school, and Hillary has had her own problems with the victim," I said. "Max, we have to consider *every* possibility."

"I guess so," my ex said as he shook his head. "How do you do it, Suzanne?"

"Do what?"

"Continually think the worst of so many people," Max said.

"I don't *always* look at folks that way," I countered.

"Maybe not, but you do when you're investigating, and you know it."

"Max, what you're failing to grasp is that you don't get *anywhere* if you wonder what the best thing is that could happen. When I'm trying to solve someone's murder, I need to think about the bad things that might drive someone to take another person's life. It's not pleasant, but it's necessary."

"And you do this for fun?" he asked me incredulously.

"I don't know if I'd say that, but there's a real sense of satisfaction making sure that nobody gets away with murder if I'm around to prevent it," I told him.

"I guess so, but I'm not sure that it's worth it."

I thought about it before I answered. "Sometimes it's not, but usually I don't have any trouble sleeping at night."

"Well, I'm glad you're suited to it, because I could never do it."

I didn't really want to discuss my psyche with my ex-husband. "Let's get back to the suspect list, Max."

He thought about it for a full minute before he spoke. "Like I said, I can see Celia, Geraldine, or Vivian stabbing Hal out of anger, and if I wasn't so sure that Karen wasn't there, she'd go on the list for sure. I warned that man about how dangerous the game he was playing was, but he wouldn't listen to me, and if I tried to push him too hard, I knew that he might pull my funding."

"So you just stood by and watched it unfold?" I asked him a little harshly.

"I never thought it would lead to murder, Suzanne! Besides, he was a grown man. If he couldn't see that what he was doing was wrong, he wasn't about to listen to me."

I backed off a bit, since he made a good point. "Do *you* think a scorned lover killed him?" I asked him.

"It's a real possibility given the way he was playing so fast and loose with those women's hearts, but then again, if he and Zane had a long-running beef, that might explain the murder as well. Wow. I just never looked at things that way before. You're right. Any one of them could have done it, and I gave the killer a golden opportunity to strike." He looked as though he wanted to cry.

"Max, if the killer hadn't stabbed Hal during those ten seconds of darkness, they would have found a way to murder him later," I told him. "All we can do now is figure out what really happened."

After striking Karen's name from our list of suspects, it still left us with five people in and around the production, which was four too many, as far as I was concerned.

"The tarts I can understand, and even Zane has his own reasons, but I still don't understand what possible motive *Hillary* would have to want to kill Hal," Max told me.

"Maybe it has something to do with the fact that she's secretly in love with Zane," I told him. "Maybe she did it to help him, or maybe even to defend him from Hal," I wondered aloud.

"What? Are you sure about that?" Max asked me.

"About what?"

"That Hillary is secretly in love with Zane," Max explained.

"I'm positive."

"Then she's got herself a problem, because I'm pretty sure Zane has been sneaking around with Geraldine Morgan on the sly for the last few weeks," Max said, dropping a new bombshell on me.

"What? What makes you say that?" I asked. I hadn't even considered that possibility, and when I thought about the two people who might or might not be romantically involved, I still had a hard time grasping it. "They aren't suited for each other at all."

"Suzanne, I know how much you pride yourself on your matchmaking skills, but you never know what will light a spark between folks when they're involved in close quarters. I first suspected it when Geraldine offered to stay late to run lines with Zane a few weeks ago. I thought she was doing it to try to make Hal jealous, and maybe that was her entire reason at first, but something clicked with them, and after a while, she wasn't playing anymore. Hal mocked her about it once in an oblique way when I was close by, but she stood her ground."

"And you were the *only* one who knew about it?" I asked, thinking of Hillary.

"They were pretty circumspect," he admitted. "Why do you ask?"

"No reason," I said.

"Celia is the one I'd be the most...Suzanne, what's going on?" he said, faltering a bit.

"Hang on a second," I told him as I held a hand up in the air. I'd had the germ of an idea for an instant, but it had vanished just as quickly as it had come. If I tried to recreate it, I knew that it would be lost to me forever, but if I ignored it, there was a good chance it would come back to me later.

"What about Celia?" I asked him to continue.

"I have no idea what I was about to say," Max admitted sheepishly.

"I'm sure you'll think of it later. So what it boils down to is that *any* of them could have done it when the lights were out," I said.

"During my ritual of darkness, you mean."

"I said what I meant, Max," I countered.

"Hey, I've seen it done before in shows I've been in, and it can be really effective."

"It also gives a killer the perfect opportunity to lash out without fear of being exposed," I told him.

"To be fair, that's the first time it's ever happened to me," Max answered.

"I should hope so." It was time to get back to my list of suspects. "Zane told me that he was standing in the wings when the lights went off. Did you see him there?" I answered.

"I might have, but if I did, it didn't register. I had other things on my mind at the time," Max admitted. He must have noticed something about my expression. "Suzanne, what's going on? Do you have something?"

"I'm not sure yet," I admitted.

"I'm not really helping, am I?" Max asked.

"You're doing fine. You've eliminated one of our main suspects, and that's nothing to sneeze at," I told him, the wheels spinning furiously in my mind. I glanced at my watch and asked, "Is there anything else?"

"Not off the top of my head, but if I think of something, I'll let you know," he told me.

I stood, and he joined me. "Thanks for stopping by the shop, Max," I said. "I'll see you at the wake."

"I'll be there. They've even got me supplying the liquor, if you can believe that," my ex said, and then he added softly, "Suzanne, you and Grace need to be careful."

"We always are," I told him glibly.

"You know what I mean. If the killer gets the idea that you two are getting close, one of you might be the next victim on their list."

"We'll be careful," I said as I touched his arm lightly. It was just like my ex-husband to do something nice like that, a gesture of real concern, that caught me off guard. Max and I had experienced a complicated relationship from the start, and it made me happy that I was with Jake now. Still, it was nice to know that he cared.

I needed to get back inside and relieve Emma, but if I had any idle time when I wasn't waiting on customers or cleaning up behind them, my ex-husband had given me a few things to think about, and there was still something nagging at the back of my conscious mind that I couldn't quite nail down. Hopefully I'd come up with it in time, but there was nothing I could do to rush the process, so I decided to get on with my life and see where it led me over the course of the next few hours.

Chapter 14

"AM I EARLY?" GRACE asked as she came into the donut shop five minutes before we were set to close.

"Just a bit, but I'll allow it," I said with a smile. "Thanks for talking to Emma last night."

She looked happy. "Did my idea work?"

"Like a charm. We made enough donuts for today, for the wake later, and for the bake sale at the school too," I told her. "Talk about your multitasking."

"How much do I owe you?" Grace asked as she pulled out her corporate checkbook.

"You know I don't feel right taking your money," I told her. "Don't sweat it. I can cover it myself."

Grace held my gaze for a few seconds, and I could see that she was deadly serious about what she was about to tell me. "Suzanne, I volunteered to cover your expenses, and that's what I mean to do. I can't make donuts, so you have to bring the talent and the equipment to the table. This is all I've got," she added as she waved her checkbook in the air. "Don't take that from me."

I could see that I wasn't going to win this particular argument. "It just seems like a lot to ask of you."

"That's the beauty of it. You're not asking. Now give me a number. I need an honest one too, so don't be cutting me any 'friends and family' discounts. Do we understand each other?"

"Sure. Let me check a few things in back, and I'll let you know," I said.

"I can live with that. In the meantime, would you like me to watch the front for you?"

"Tell you what. If anyone comes in, give me a yell," I told her.

"You don't trust me?" Grace asked me innocently.

"It's not a matter of trust. It's just that I like to be the one in charge."

"You don't have to tell me that," she answered with a grin.

I walked back into the kitchen and headed for my tiny little office.

"What's up?" Emma asked me as she finished sweeping the floor in back.

"Grace needs to know how much our expenses are for the extra projects we did today," I explained.

Emma smiled as she handed me a sheet listing the extra supplies we'd used and their approximate cost as well. "I already made one up for her. I hope you don't mind."

"Why should I mind?" I asked her as I studied it. Emma had come close to the figure I'd had in mind, which made me feel good about my business sense. After all, I'd learned early on that if I took care of the pennies, the dollars would follow suit. It was a lesson Momma had drilled into me when I'd been younger and one I was eternally grateful for. "This looks good. What made you do one on your own?" I asked out of idle curiosity more than anything else.

"Grace might have mentioned needing one last night when we chatted," she admitted. "Sorry. I should have said something to you before now."

"Don't worry about it, Emma. Thanks for saving me the trouble." I tapped the sheet. "This is right on the money, isn't it? You didn't give her a single discount, did you?"

My assistant shook her head as she explained, "I was going to, but she told me she'd know if I tried to cut her any slack, and I believed her. Suzanne, she couldn't *really* know, could she?"

"I wouldn't put it past her," I said. "Thanks for doing this. Let's go ahead and close up a few minutes early. You can grab the few donuts left up front and add them to the stack I'm taking to the wake. That should make cleanup a little bit easier."

"I'm on it," she said.

"It seems you already asked Emma for this last night," I told Grace as I handed her the sheet. "Why didn't you just get it from her instead of asking me for one?"

Grace shrugged. "I figured if she'd told you about it, you would have mentioned it first thing. Sorry if I interrupted the chain of command."

"I'm not running a battle group," I told her. "The truth is that Emma and her mother know just about as much about running Donut Hearts as I do."

"You should be proud of that," she said. "That means you trained them well."

As she wrote out the check, I said, "While you're doing that, I'll get started on shutting everything down for the day."

I locked the front door, an easy thing to do since we had no customers at the moment, and as I ran the register reports, I totaled up the cash drawer. After that, it went like clockwork buttoning everything up, especially since Emma was working right along beside me. The two of us were a well-oiled machine. I still loved the single day a week I ran the shop alone, but the days I usually treasured were the ones with Emma, especially now that I didn't know how long I'd have her with me. As the restaurant grew more from an idea into a reality, I knew full well that I might lose her after it opened. I could live with that, but that didn't mean that I was in any hurry to make it happen, either.

I was about to make out the deposit slip for the bank when Grace said, "Don't forget to add this to your bottom line," as she waved the check toward me.

I grabbed it as I said, "Thanks again for doing this." I was jotting the number down on the deposit slip when I noticed that she'd made a mistake. "This isn't right."

"Why, isn't it enough?" she asked me with a grin.

"It's double what we asked you for, and you know it," I told her with a stern expression of my own. It was all I could do to accept any money from her at all, but there was no way in the world I was going to allow her to double it.

"Suzanne, it *has* to be that amount," she insisted.

"I can tear it up and you can write me another one, or we can just forget about you contributing anything at all. It's your choice," I said as I started to tear the check up.

"Don't do that!" she said loudly enough to startle me and pull Emma out of the kitchen.

"Is everything all right up here?" she asked as she looked from one of us to the other.

"We're having a little disagreement," I told her, not taking my gaze off my best friend. "Everything's fine."

"Okay then," Emma answered quickly as she ducked back into the kitchen. I was sure she didn't want any part of this situation, and I couldn't blame her. It wasn't often that Grace and I clashed, but that didn't mean that we *never* did.

"Suzanne, I *have* to pay you double," Grace said, almost pleading with me.

"Why do you *have* to?" I asked her, curious to hear what possible rationale she could have for saying such a thing.

"I'm under budget on my corporate account, and if I don't spend enough by Friday, they're going to cut it next quarter," she explained.

"That's too bad, but it still doesn't justify me taking more than I deserve," I said, unwilling to compromise.

"Hang on a second," she said as she held up the list of items we'd used. "This covers supplies, but it doesn't touch your time, or Emma's either, not to mention the wear and tear on your equipment or the utilities, or anything like that."

"You don't need to worry about those things," I said.

Grace frowned at me for a moment before she spoke again. "Can't you just cash that check as a favor to me? Isn't that what friends are for? I don't ask you for much, but this is important to me."

I could see that she was deadly serious, and while I had my pride, I didn't want it to cost me my relationship with Grace. "Thank you," I said as I endorsed the check and added the hefty amount to my deposit.

"I should be the one thanking you, and Grace too," she said. "My boss absolutely loved the idea of supporting the school system and the arts all in the same day. She kept going on and on about how well I'm doing."

I shook my head. "You are in a crazy business. You know that, don't you? I can't think of anywhere else you get praised for spending more money than you need to."

"You get up in the middle of the night to make donuts, and *I'm* the one who is in a crazy business?" she asked with a laugh.

"That's a fair point, I suppose," I said.

Emma poked her head out of the kitchen. "Is it safe to come out yet?"

"It's all clear. We've put our sabers away," I told her with a smile.

"Good. I hate when two of my mommies fight."

"Don't you have somewhere you need to be?" I asked her with a grin.

"On my way, boss," she said as she headed for the door. "Thanks again for covering things for the bake sale, Grace."

"Happy to do it," she replied.

After she was gone, Grace asked, "How long do you think she'll stay after they open that restaurant of Barton's?"

"I've been thinking about it, and I finally decided that I don't want to even consider the possibility of her ever leaving me," I said firmly. "Let's go get some lunch, shall we?"

"Not before we go to the bank," Grace said. "I don't want to give you a chance to talk me out of that check."

"You know me too well, don't you?" I asked her with a smile.

"I don't know about that. I'd say I know you just the right amount," she answered, and I had to agree.

The front was finished, and in the kitchen, we had rows of boxes ready for the wake, but for now, I needed something to eat.

After I went by the bank, of course.

"Do you have a place for us to sit?" I asked Trish as I looked around the crowded diner. The café was brimming with people, and I was afraid we might have to get our food to go.

"Give me one second," Trish said as she moved away from the register into the dining area.

"Don't evict anyone on our account," I told her.

Trish frowned. "Wow, you take all of the fun out of it," she said as she stopped in her tracks.

Just then, I heard someone calling my name. It was Paige Hill, owner of our bookstore, and one of my best friends in April Springs. "Suzanne," she repeated. "Why don't you two join me?"

"There you go. Ask and it shall be given," Trish said. "I'll be over in a few minutes."

"We can save you a trip," I said. "Two burgers, two fries, and two sweet teas, please." Then I turned to Grace before she could say anything and asked, "Would you like anything?"

All three of us started laughing. "You can share all of that with me, you greedy girl," Grace said. Things had been a little tense between us back at the donut shop, but we were right as rain again, which was the most important thing to me in the world.

"Okay, fine. I'll share," I replied.

"See you soon," Trish replied as a man at the register started clearing his throat. "Judge, you'd better have a tickle in your throat, because if you're trying to hurry me up, you're in a world of hurt, sir."

"Show some respect, young lady," Judge Hurley said.

"I called you sir, didn't I?" she asked.

"That you did. Take your time. I'm not due back in court for another..." He glanced at his watch and then said, "Six minutes."

"Don't you worry. I'll get you out in time," she told him as Grace and I made our way back to Paige's table.

"Thanks for making room for us," I said as we sat with her.

"I just wish I could stay and chat, but we've got a shipment coming in today that I have to sign for," she replied. "Ever since Rita made a mistake signing for a box of graphic novels we didn't order, she hates to agree to accept anything."

"Do you mean comic books?" Grace asked her.

"Get with the times, girl," Paige said. "We're not talking about Archie and Jughead here. These things can be really dark."

"No thank you," Grace said.

"Me, either. I'll stick with my mysteries," I added.

"Speaking of which, how's that book club of yours doing?" Paige must have seen the expression on my face, because she quickly added, "Strike that. I have high hopes that someday, I'll be able to mind my own business, all evidence to the contrary so far."

"You're fine," I said. "Everyone has busy lives, but we've got plans to start up again in the autumn once the weather starts to cool off again."

"That's a long time to wait. In the meantime, you're always welcome to join one of my groups," Paige said as her phone rang. "Hang on," she said as she answered it. "Yes. I'm coming. Right now. Rita, just sign! Okay, I'm sorry I raised my voice. I'll be right there." Paige shrugged and turned to us. "The joys of running a small business. Am I right?"

"As rain," I said.

Once she was gone, Trish showed up with our sweet teas and cleaned the table for us. "Burgers will be out in a second," she said before heading back up front quickly.

"Wow, I wouldn't like to do what she does every day," Grace said as we saw her ring up three customers and deliver an order in between.

"I couldn't handle it either," I said. "I've found my niche, and I'm glad that Trish found hers, but neither one of us would trade places for the day, even for a big fat check at the end of it."

"You two keep on being entrepreneurs," Grace said with a smile. "And I'll keep on doing what I'm doing."

"Being a patron of the arts as well as the local school system?" I asked her with a grin.

"Among other things," she said. "Is there anything new with the investigation that I need to know about?"

"As a matter of fact, there is," I said. I could see how Max had forgotten to mention his little blackout to us before. Things did seem to happen quickly. "Max turned off the lights for ten seconds before the performance to put them all in the mood for what was to come. I've been wondering how someone could so blatantly stab Hal and no one see it, so that explains that. Also, it turns out that Karen Lexington has an alibi, so we have to take her off our list."

"What?" She was about to ask for details when she spotted Trish approaching with our burgers. "Wait until after lunch. This place is too crowded to compare notes in anyway."

"Agreed," I said.

After Trish brought us our food, we ate, chatting about nothing in particular. We were nearly finished when I heard someone talking behind us about the murder. She must not have seen us come into the diner, because she didn't bother trying to keep her voice down.

"I know who killed Hal Embry, and if the police don't figure it out pretty soon, I'm going to blow this thing wide open."

Chapter 15

IT TOOK ALL I HAD IN me not to turn and stare at the woman who was speaking. It was clear to me that it was Vivian Crowe, but who exactly was she talking to? I risked a quick glance and saw why she hadn't seen us. Her back was turned to our table, so there was a good chance she didn't even realize that Grace and I had come into the Boxcar Grill. Vivian was with a woman I didn't recognize, but I didn't know everyone in April Springs, contrary to popular belief.

"Don't keep me in suspense," the woman said. "Who did it?"

Vivian hesitated before responding. "I'm not going to say anything until I confront them at the wake," she said. "I don't want to take any chances."

That was the worst idea I'd ever heard in my life. I reached over and tapped her on the shoulder. "Vivian, that's a good way to die."

"Suzanne? What are you talking about?"

"Tell us who you suspect and why, and let us handle it," I told her.

"You and your sidekick there?" Vivian asked me scornfully. "I've heard all about your reputations for being investigators, but you two shouldn't believe your own hype. I'm just as capable of solving this as you are."

"Is it really worth taking the chance?" I asked her.

"The room is going to be crowded with people," she said, dismissing my warning. "No one would dare raise a hand to me."

"The stage was also crowded when Hal Embry was murdered," I reminded her.

"That was different. It was dark then, or did you not know that?" she asked, though it was clear she wasn't as sure as she had been a moment earlier.

"We know all about that," I told her.

Grace spoke up. "Vivian, the truth is that we've come close to dying more times than we'd care to admit. It's a dangerous thing to do, trying to unmask a killer. They don't always sit there and take it. The most dangerous folks we've run into were the ones who felt as though they were cornered and had no way out."

"Perhaps you're right," she conceded.

"Again, who do you suspect and why?" I asked her urgently. If she had some insights that we didn't, knowing everyone involved in the case better than we did, I wanted to hear her thoughts.

"If what you just said is true, why should I let you risk *your* lives?" she asked. "I don't want your blood on my hands." She shivered slightly as she added that last bit.

"Because we've survived it before," I told her.

"That's not exactly encouraging," Vivian answered.

"Then tell the police," I blurted out. Sure, I would have loved to solve the murder with Grace, but as long as the killer was caught, that was all that really mattered to me.

"It would still get back to the murderer," Vivian said. She pondered for a moment or two more before adding, "I don't care what Darby Jones says. I'm getting out of here right now, and he's going to have to lock me up to stop me."

Vivian stood to leave, and I followed her. Grace thrust some money at Trish on our way out, and we stopped Vivian in the parking lot. "Hang on a second."

"Suzanne, you think you're so clever, but I know that *you* called the police before and told them I was leaving town," she said as she turned on me. "See? You can't keep a secret in this town."

"Running away isn't going to solve anything," I told her.

Vivian's laugh was almost on the edge of hysteria. "You've got to be kidding. If the murderer can't find me, then they can't kill me next. That's simple enough."

"Okay, so you're leaving. I won't try to stop you again," I told her.

"Thank you."

"If..." I said, letting that one word hang in the air for a few seconds. "If you tell me right now who it is that you suspect. Like you said, what does it matter if the killer finds out you said something? You'll be long gone by then."

"Fine, but I'm washing my hands of your blood if you do anything stupid and get yourself killed," she said.

"I can live with that," I acknowledged. "So, who is it?"

"Officer Rick Handler," she said, and then she started to get into her car.

"Rick Handler?" I asked, blocking her way.

"Yes," she admitted. "That's really why I haven't gone to the police, and it's why I'm begging you not to go to them, either. Suzanne, Grace, my life is in your hands."

"Why would Rick kill Hal?" Grace asked.

"We know that he's Karen's nephew, but that doesn't make him a killer," I told her.

"Ask him why he was lurking around the theater when the murder occurred, then," she said. "Now I've got to go. Don't tell anyone I'm gone. Please."

We watched her drive away, and Grace made a move for her phone.

"Who are you calling?" I asked her.

"Darby," she admitted.

"Hang on a second," I said. "Let's go talk to Rick first."

"If he killed Hal, he's going to be dangerous," Grace said.

"That's why we're going to see if he's at the police station," I said.

We walked over, leaving my Jeep in Trish's crowded parking lot. That was one of the good things about living in a small town. Everything was close to everything else. I headed for the station with Grace beside me.

"What if he's not there?" she asked me.

"Then we talk to Darby and convince him to call him in," I admitted.

It took him a few minutes to come out to the front after we checked with the dispatcher, but Rick Handler came out, looking confused. "What do you need to speak with me for?" he asked.

"We need to ask you and Darby a question, and it has to be together," Grace said.

"Do you mean Acting Chief of Police Jones?" he asked her with a frown.

"You know who I'm talking about," she said.

"What's this about, Grace?"

"It's Mrs. Grant to you, as in the chief of police's wife," Grace said icily. "Now are we going to go see Officer Jones now, or are we going to do it *after* I recall a very angry husband from his vacation?"

"Fine. Acting Chief Jones is in his office," Officer Handler replied a little stiffly.

"What's going on?" Darby asked us as the three of us walked into his office.

"I have no idea. It's their show," Officer Handler said as he pointed to us.

"Why were you at the theater the night of the dress rehearsal?" I asked him.

"That's why you're here? Seriously?" Rick Handler asked us. "I was working."

"That's not strictly true," Darby said as he frowned at his friend and fellow law officer. "You were off duty."

"I didn't say I was working for the department," Handler quickly explained. "Max sometimes hires me to help him with the sets. It's a way to pick up some extra cash, and it never interferes with my police work," Handler said. "Anyway, I was there because he wanted some last-minute changes to the set design."

"Why am I just hearing about this?" Darby asked him.

"Hey, it's not something I really want getting around, you know? I'm supposed to be this tough cop, not an interior designer."

"I don't know why you couldn't be both," I said. "You don't have to be weak or less than anything to be artistic."

"Maybe, but you're not a cop, so you wouldn't understand," Handler said.

"Were you in uniform at the auditorium? Did you have your firearm on you?" Darby asked him.

"No to both questions," Handler said. "I had a paintbrush. That was the most dangerous thing on me."

"I don't see a problem then," Darby said. "Why are you two making such a fuss about it?"

"We have an eyewitness that saw you lurking in the shadows at the dress rehearsal the night of the murder," I said, doubting now that the information we'd gotten from Vivian had been any good.

"I brought Max some paint samples, but I was long gone by the time Hal was murdered," Officer Handler said. "Chief, I'd appreciate it if you'd keep my moonlighting job to yourself."

"What moonlighting job?" Darby asked him with a grin. "Now, don't you have an area to patrol, Officer?"

"Yes, sir," Officer Handler said with a slight grin, and then he left, shooting us each a sideways glance as he did so.

"I'm sorry," I started to say to Darby when he held up a hand.

"One second. Suzanne, what's Max's telephone number?"

I gave it to him, and when he got an answer, he asked, "Max, was Rick Handler at the auditorium the night of the murder? Okay. When did he leave? Are you sure about that? It's nothing. Thanks. Talk to you later." After he hung up, he shrugged. "He just confirmed Rick's story. He came by, got the samples, and then he snuck out the back before anyone saw him there, or so he thought. Max says that there is no way Rick was there at the time of the murder."

"Then someone needs to stop Vivian Crowe from leaving town again," I told him. "She just took off again."

"Let her go," the acting chief of police said.

"Seriously? Just like that?" Grace asked him.

"She didn't do it," he said. "Why shouldn't she be able to come and go as she sees fit?"

"How could she possibly have an alibi?" I asked him. We hadn't heard a word about that, and we'd been asking quite a few folks some very tough questions.

"It turns out that she wasn't in the blackout circle after all," he told us. "She was outside sneaking a cigarette, and one of the lighting crew was out there with her. They alibied each other, so her name's off the list."

"They could have done it together," Grace suggested.

"Harvey Nations? Seriously? He had no motive at all, and besides, Jimmy Wilkes saw them out there the entire time. He was playing with his new telescope on the roof of the bank building, and he happened to spot them. I had a talk with him about keeping that thing pointed skyward and not around town, but it confirms it. Vivian didn't do it, and neither did Harvey."

"We didn't even have him on our list," I admitted.

"Then that will save you the trouble of marking it off," he told us. "Have you ladies uncovered any other smoking-hot leads for me?" He asked the question with a bit of derision in his voice, so I was in no mood to share anything else with him.

"No," I said, and Grace agreed. "When were you going to tell us about Vivian?"

"Truthfully, I haven't had time to turn around since Hal Embry got himself murdered," Darby admitted. "Sorry. I should have told you."

"That's okay," I said. "Now if you'll excuse us, we have a few things to do before the wake. Will we see you at the donut shop before we go?"

"I'm trying to make that happen, but it's too soon to say," he told us.

"Well, we're leaving around quarter till three, so if you're going with us, you need to be at the donut shop by then," I told him. "Come on, Grace. Let's get out of his hair."

"At least your hearts were in the right place," Darby told us.

If that was an apology for withholding information from us, it needed some work.

Once we were outside, Grace asked me, "Do you believe him?"

"We don't have any reason not to," I admitted. "I still think someone should tell Vivian that what she saw was perfectly innocent."

"How do we manage that, though?"

"I've got her cell phone number. Let me call her," I said.

It went straight to voicemail, which led me to believe that either her phone was off or she was ignoring me. The least I could do was leave her a message, though.

"Vivian, Rick Handler has an alibi, so he is in the clear, and so are you. There's no reason to run. We found out you were sneaking a cigarette outside when the murder occurred. Call me if you have any questions. This is Suzanne Hart, by the way."

"That's the best I can do for now," I told her.

"So, we're down to four suspects," Grace said. "Two tarts, an understudy, and a costumer."

"I think they prefer to be called wardrobe supervisors," I said.

"I don't care if they want to all be known as Flying Nuns. You know what I mean."

"I do," I agreed. I glanced at my watch. "We don't have much time left before we have to leave for the wake. What do you want to do before we have to head back to Donut Hearts?"

"We could always confront one of our remaining suspects," she suggested.

"We could do that, but Geraldine is probably in Union Square, Zane Whitlow is decidedly unhappy with us at the moment, and Celia Laslow is in Maple Hollow. That leaves Hillary Teal. At least she doesn't hate us."

"Not yet, at any rate," Grace said. "Hillary it is, then."

Chapter 16

"HILLARY, DO YOU HAVE a second?" I asked her when she answered her front door. The poor woman looked as though she'd been crying. "Are you okay?"

"I'm fine," she said, clearly lying.

"You're obviously not," I said. "Is it something you'd like to talk about?"

"Yes. No. I don't know," she answered.

"Hillary, it might do you some good to get it off your chest," Grace said. "Why don't we come in and sit down?"

The costumer seemed to consider it, and then she said, "I don't suppose it can hurt anything at this point."

We followed her into her living room, which was covered by doilies in every direction. There was plastic on all of the furniture, and in general, the place had a rather unlived-in look. As I sat on the couch across from the chair, the plastic crinkled and creaked under me, but if Hillary noticed, she didn't say anything. Grace's eyebrows shot up though, but that ended the moment she sat beside me, replicating the sound herself.

"Is this about Hal Embry?" I asked her once we were settled.

"No. You'd think so, but at the moment, I'm allowing my personal feelings to get in the way of my mourning." She crossed her legs at the ankle and clasped her hands together in her lap. "Where are my manners? I'll make us all some tea."

"Thanks, but we just came from lunch," I told her. I knew that the offer was more of a distraction for her than a hostess chore, but I wasn't going to let her delay talking to us if I could help it. "What happened, if this isn't related to Hal?"

"I just found out an hour ago that I've been a fool for several weeks now," she said, and then she burst out crying.

I got up and moved toward her, touching her shoulder lightly. "I'm so sorry," I said. "What did you find out?"

"Zane doesn't care about me. He is in love with Geraldine Morgan," she said. "It was going on right under my nose, but I was too blind to see it."

"How did you find out about them?" I asked her.

"I saw them at his house," she said, talking softly through her tears. "I'm acting like an idiot, aren't I? Here I am a grown woman, and I'm acting as though I'm some kind of heartbroken teenager."

"We all feel pain, no matter our age," Grace told her.

"That's true enough. I'm certainly feeling it right now," Hillary responded.

"Was there a scene?" I asked her, getting her back on track.

"No, I slunk away like some kind of timid little mouse, which is what I suppose I am and will always be," she answered. "I peeked in through the blinds to make sure it wasn't a bad time to surprise him, and I saw them on the couch together."

"Did they see you?" I asked her.

"No, they were so...occupied with each other that they didn't even notice me. I should have pounded on the door and demanded an explanation, but of course I would never have the nerve to do that. Instead, I scampered back here, blinded by my tears and sorrow, and pulled the hole in after myself."

"Hillary, you can't blame yourself for missing the signs. They were clearly very clever about covering their affair up," I told her.

"Did you two know about this? You don't seem at all surprised," she stated as she frowned at us in turn.

"We heard a rumor about it today," I admitted, "but until that moment, we had no idea."

"It appears they are *both* very good at disguising their behavior," she answered, accepting my answer. I was worried for a moment that she might think of me as a coconspirator in the affair, but even if she had,

I doubted she would have done much about it; it just didn't seem to be in her nature.

"What are you going to do?" Grace asked her. "Are you still going to the wake for Hal Embry?"

"What? Of course not! I'd never be able to face either one of them after the fool I've made of myself." She shivered a bit as she said it, as though a shade had walked across her grave.

I couldn't blame her for her initial reaction of deciding not to go, but I felt as though I needed to say something. "Do you know what I'd do if I were you?" I asked her.

"Leave town and never look back?" she asked me with a timid little smile.

"Certainly not as Plan A, or Plan B either, for that matter," I said, happy that she could at least tease about it. "I would dry my tears, put on my prettiest dress, and then I'd go to that wake and do my level best to forget all about Zane Whitlow and Geraldine Morgan."

"I would do the exact same thing myself," Grace chipped in.

"I'm sure that you both would, but I'm not half as brave as either one of you are," she said.

"Hillary, the only way you can really lose is if you let this keep you from doing what you must do. You liked Hal, didn't you?"

"I respected him as an actor," she admitted. "I can't believe he's gone. I wish..."

"What do you wish?" I asked.

"Never mind. I'd give anything to make it all just go away, but it doesn't matter now. It's too late to change anything. He's gone, and I'm so sorry it happened that I can't stand it."

"Then doesn't he deserve your presence at his farewell?" Grace asked.

"I don't know. I should go; I know you're right. If I don't, I'll regret it for the rest of my life," Hillary said so softly I could barely hear her.

"Then you need to do what your heart tells you to do," I said.

"I'll try," she said, letting a deep breath escape her lungs. "I understand that you two are catering the event. If I falter, may I lean on you?"

"Of course you can," I said, feeling real sympathy for the woman. Her situation was nowhere near the same as mine had been when I'd found out that Max had cheated on me, but no one deserved a broken heart.

"Then I must prepare myself," Hillary said as she stood.

"One more thing before we go," I said, remembering why we'd come by in the first place. "Do you have any idea as to who might have killed Hal Embry?"

She noticeably shivered. "I've been trying not to think about it. It's like some kind of bad dream that I keep hoping I'll wake up from."

She'd hesitated before saying that, though, and Grace must have sensed it as well. "You can tell us anything. We will be discreet."

"Well, I shouldn't say anything, but you've both been so kind to me this afternoon." Hillary took a deep breath, and then she said, "If I were to suspect anyone, it would be Celia Laslow."

"Celia? Why?" I asked her. While it was true Celia was on our list of suspects, we hadn't been able to pin a strong enough motive to her so far.

"She confided in me last week that she believed Hal was about to propose to her when she found out he'd been seeing the other women as well," Hillary said softly. "She was furious."

"We'll look into it," I promised her.

"Besides, there's something people seem to keep forgetting," Hillary mentioned.

"What's that?"

"Celia's the one who discovered that Hal was dead in the first place," she said. "If you ask me, she seemed to be overacting when she shrieked out his real name. I wondered from the very start if she might have had something to do with it and was trying to cover her tracks. Who better than the woman who was supposed to stab him in the script in the first place? If you ask me, I believe that she took her cue from her character, and she killed him while no one else was looking," Hillary added.

"Can you prove any of that?" I asked her.

"Call Max. He knows that script frontwards and backwards. He'll tell you that in the play, Celia is the real killer, and in this case, life imitated art."

"Max, who's the killer?" I asked once we were back outside and I had him on the phone.

"Why ask me? I thought you two were digging into it," he said.

"In the play," I said strongly.

"Oh, Jenny did it," he said.

"Let me guess. Celia Laslow played the role of Jenny, am I right?"

"Yeah, but you don't get any credit for guessing that. After all, you had a one in three chance of getting it right."

"That's the thing, though," I told him. "I wasn't guessing."

Chapter 17

"WHAT ARE YOU TALKING about, Suzanne?" Max asked me.

"I'll tell you later," I said. He was still talking when I hung up on him, but I didn't really feel like explaining myself. Max had just confirmed part of what Hillary had told us, and he'd been the one who'd first brought up the affair between Geraldine and Zane. Could the costumer be right about Celia? We'd have to take a harder and longer look at the actress from Maple Hollow, but there was no time to try to run her down at the moment.

Grace and I needed to get back to Donut Hearts and collect the food for the wake, and possibly even the acting chief of police as well.

It was going to be an interesting time, to say the least.

"How long have you been waiting for us?" I asked Officer Darby Jones when I got out of the Jeep.

"I just got here," he admitted.

"Where did you park your cruiser?" Grace asked him.

"I didn't want to rouse any suspicions, so I walked over from the station. Let me inside, okay? I don't want to be seen out here talking to you two."

I grinned at Grace. "It's not the first time we've heard that, is it?"

"Not the second, either," she said with a smile of her own.

"You know what I mean," he answered, his voice a little on edge.

"Of course we do, but how are you going to sneak into the theater? You can't exactly do that without being spotted," I told him as I let him inside.

"You're going to unlock the stage door in back and let me in," Darby told me.

"I can do that," I answered.

"Does that mean that you're not going to help us carry the donuts in?" Grace asked him.

He started sputtering. "How can I keep a low profile and do that? I thought you understood that I'd be hiding in the wings."

I glanced over and saw Grace grinning at him. "She's just pulling your chain, Darby. May I still call you Darby in private, or do you need your official title even here?"

"We should use it, and curtsey too," Grace said.

"I'm not sure I remember how," I answered.

"It's easy. Just do it with a sweeping motion," she replied, and then she did as she'd promised. When I'd tried it as a kid, I'd nearly fallen over, my balance was so bad, but Grace looked like an absolute princess.

"Have you been practicing?" I asked her.

"I may have watched *The Crown* on Netflix and tried to replicate it a few times," she admitted.

"Can we get moving?" Darby asked.

"Yes, Your Royal Highness," I said. I nearly toppled again, but I did manage a curtsey of my own, though it wasn't executed nearly as well as Grace's had been.

"Do you two ever get tired of trying to be funny all of the time?" he asked.

"Try? Did you just say try?" Grace replied.

"Can we back up a few minutes and let me start over?" Darby begged.

"He's under a lot of stress," I told Grace. "Let's leave the poor man alone."

"We could, but then what fun would that be?" my best friend said, and then she nodded. "You're right." After turning to Darby, she added, "Sorry. We get carried away sometimes. It helps break the tension."

"I'm the first to admit that we could all use that, but we've got to be on top of things this afternoon. Don't ever forget there's a killer on the loose."

I stood in front of him and said solemnly, "Darby, don't ever think that just because we tease and joke that we don't take this deadly serious. We've come too close too many times to being killed ourselves to ever forget that."

"Okay, fine. As long as we're all on the same page," he said. "Are you going to pull your Jeep around back so you can load the donuts out of sight?"

"*I'm* not hiding anything," I told him. "Tell you what. I'll go unlock the doors, and you can crawl in back. We'll load the donuts, and no one will be the wiser that you're there."

"It sounds a little melodramatic when you put it that way, doesn't it?" Darby admitted.

"No," Grace answered for me. "You've got a point. If folks know you're in the wings during the wake, they might not be as free with their comments. I hope someone brings some booze to this thing."

"Got a hankering for some liquor?" I asked Grace with a slight tilt of my head.

"No, but if they get a little drunk, it can't do anything but help our cause," she said.

"Don't worry. Max is making sure that there are spirits supplied," I assured her.

"How can you be sure of that?" Darby asked. "After all, it's not even three o'clock in the afternoon right now."

"Yes, but I doubt anyone there will care about that. They're going to say goodbye to a fellow actor struck down in the middle of a performance. Can you imagine any occasion that merited a final toast more than that? They've already asked him, and he's agreed to do it."

"Then maybe the booze will loosen up some lips," Grace said. She turned to Darby and said, "Come on, Acting Chief of Police Jones. Let's sneak you into the back of Suzanne's Jeep."

Once we had him situated, I looked around to see if anyone had been paying attention to us as we'd maneuvered Darby into the vehicle.

There was a complete lack of interest or even notice from the few people who were out and about in the middle of a warm day. As Grace and I started carrying donuts out to put in the back, I realized that we had way too many for the wake. Paige came out from her bookstore across the street and waved to me.

"Going somewhere special with all of those treats?" she called out.

I made a sudden executive decision and grabbed one of the full boxes. As I walked across Springs Drive, I said, "I've got some goodies for you."

"Wow, that's the best offer I've had all week," she answered. "I trust these are extras."

"They are," I admitted. "Is that okay with you?"

"Are you kidding? It's fantastic," Paige said as she eagerly took the box from me. "You are a life saver," she told me as she nipped the tape with a fingernail and looked inside. "I just love your goodies."

"I'm glad," I said.

Grace glanced at her watch and said, "Hey, Paige. Suzanne, we're going to be late."

"So you are going somewhere," Paige said.

"We're catering Hal Embry's wake," I admitted.

The bookstore owner suddenly looked a bit less enthusiastic about the box of treats she was now holding. "Were these meant for...you know?"

"No, they were part of our overrun for the day," I lied to her. What did it matter *why* I'd made them? I figured what she didn't know wouldn't hurt her. Then again, the donuts I'd given her *may* have actually been extras from the shop. I couldn't say for sure one way or the other, so I wasn't lying to her about their origins.

"They smell amazing, so I'm going to choose to believe you," she said after a moment.

"I appreciate that. Well, I've got to run."

"Thanks again," she said as she waved to me with her free hand.

"You bet," I told her.

"It's about time you showed up," Geraldine Morgan said as I drove up to the front of the auditorium after stopping to let Darby out near the back entrance.

I glanced at my watch. "I don't know what you're talking about. We're early," I told her.

"Perhaps, but people are already starting to gather inside," she intoned.

"Feel free to cut my fee in half," I told her as I shoved a few boxes into her unwilling hands. "Oh, that's right, I'm donating these free of charge."

There must have been even more sting in my tone than in my words, because Geraldine quickly backtracked. "I'm sorry. Something happened earlier that's put me in a bad mood."

"More than attending a wake for your costar?" Grace asked her as she grabbed a few boxes herself.

"That is certainly tragic enough, but I'm talking about something else entirely. I would tell you, but it's too personal to share."

She looked a bit smug, as though she knew something we didn't. After her earlier comment, I couldn't let it just slide. "Is it about the affair you're having with Zane Whitlow, or the fact that Hillary Whitlow knows all about it?"

"*Hillary* knows?" Geraldine snapped. "That's impossible. We've been so careful."

"Here's a tip from your friendly neighborhood donut maker. Close the blinds if you're going to canoodle on the couch."

Her face went ashen. "She saw us?"

"She did," I said.

"I need to find her and apologize," Geraldine said. "I had no idea that she had a crush on Zane until a bit ago. She must be shattered."

"I'm not sure apologizing right now is the best course of action," I said, but I realized that she couldn't possibly care less about my opinion. Geraldine hurried into the auditorium, and Grace and I followed after I collected a few more boxes of goodies. That would give us almost a hundred donuts, surely enough for the small crowd that would be gathering there. That left three dozen in the back of my Jeep, so I was glad that I'd given Paige a box. I might be playing the donut fairy after this was over, delivering donuts to folks who weren't expecting them.

"Let's go see what happens," Grace said as she led the way.

When we walked in, I saw Geraldine hurrying onto the stage and heading right toward Hillary Teal, who was in deep conversation with Zane Whitlow, the unlikely Lothario at the heart of this particular love triangle.

Something must have been said that I couldn't catch from where I stood, because Hillary stared at him for a moment and started to cry, and then she bolted off the stage.

"Here," I said as I piled my boxes on top of Grace's. "Take these."

She juggled them for a moment before they settled in, but I barely noticed. Hillary needed someone to talk to, and I wasn't about to let her down, especially since I'd been the one, along with Grace, who had convinced her to come.

"Hillary, wait a second," I said as she started up the far aisle of the theater.

"I can't do it, Suzanne," she said haltingly.

"Are you okay?" I asked lamely. It was hard to know what might be the right thing to say in a moment like that, but that was the best I could do.

"I need to be alone," she said.

"No, what you need to do is to stay here," I told her. After all, her pain wouldn't lessen by being absent from its cause. Hillary had to face this or be haunted by it for the rest of her life.

"You can't tell me what to do," Hillary snapped, and I saw a hint of anger in her gaze. Good. Maybe a little bit of a tantrum would do her some good.

"I'm not trying to, but you still can't leave. I've got something I need to talk to you about, and it can't wait." That wasn't exactly true, but I needed her to face her anger and resentment, not bury it, so I had to say *something* to make her hang around.

Hillary looked at me with a moment of fear in her eyes, shook her head, and then she ran out of the auditorium without another word. Why on earth would she be afraid of me giving her a pep talk? Her spirit had gone from fighting to assert itself to being completely absent the next moment, all because of me. I hadn't meant to be so stern with her, and I started after her so I could apologize when Grace walked up beside me.

"Let her go, Suzanne," she said. "Don't forget about Darby."

In all of the excitement, I'd done just that. The acting chief of police had been standing outside in the heat, waiting for me to let him in, and I'd been so focused on the drama before me that I'd forgotten all about him. I decided that I'd track Hillary down later and apologize to her, but at the moment, I had something quite a bit more pressing to do.

"You're right. Sorry about that," I said as I took two boxes back and headed for the stage. "Was I too hard on Hillary just now?"

"No, she needs to face reality and stop living in some dream world she's created for herself," Grace reassured me.

"I'm still going to apologize to her," I told her. "You know that, right?"

"Now tell me something I don't know," Grace said with a gentle grin. "You just can't do it this very moment."

"No, but it has to be sooner rather than later," I said as I placed my boxes on the table. I noticed that Max had indeed provided alcohol for the event. I couldn't believe it, but I was happy to see that most of the folks gathered already had full glasses in their hands. At least maybe my donuts would soak up some of the booze so no one got too hammered so early in the day.

I worked my way back to the rear stage door, and fortunately, no one noticed me as Grace made a display of nearly dropping one of her boxes to give me the distraction I needed. We hadn't even planned it out, but we'd been working together so long on these cases that some of it was instinctual, like a kind of detective muscle memory.

"Where have you been?" Darby asked, sweating as he wiped his brow.

"I got held up," I told him, not having any desire to stand there and be scolded. Was I wearing some kind of sign on my forehead that said "Pick on me"? If so, it was a bad day for anyone who decided to follow up on it.

Without another word I rejoined the group. Grace was opening boxes as fast as she could, and the crowd descended on my treats like locusts on a fresh crop. Maybe I hadn't made enough after all, as I saw Celia stuff a few extras into her oversized purse. I might have said something to her, but the truth was she was doing me a favor. I hated to see my goodies go to waste, even if it meant one of the actors in the play absconded with more than her share.

Max looked around and then stepped into the center of the stage. Even I had to admit that he had a real presence there. He was tall and handsome, there was no denying that, but he also had something about him, an aura that demanded attention and got it. My ex-husband held up his plastic glass and said,

"To Hal.

May our memories of you linger sweet and be long.

May our thoughts of you be filled with joy and with song.

May your light shine true through right and through wrong.

And may your name be remembered among us, where it will always belong.

Let us raise our glasses to our fallen friend, Hal Embry, an actor."

I wondered where Max had stolen his toast. No matter; it was a nice way to say good-bye, and there weren't many dry eyes on that stage. It wasn't the eulogy so much as it was the way Max had delivered it.

After that, people broke up into smaller groups.

And that's when the whole thing started getting really interesting.

Chapter 18

GRACE AND I HAD WORKED our way off the stage so we could keep an eye on everyone there from the audience. As we took seats seven rows back from the front, we could see them all clearly, but they couldn't see us.

"All we need now is some popcorn," Grace whispered to me.

"And soda," I added softly.

"Look over there," she said suddenly, but I didn't need her prompt. The loud voices were enough to draw our—and everyone else's—attention.

"You couldn't control yourself, could you?" Celia yelled at Geraldine. "First you went after Hal, and when you couldn't get him, you set your sights on his understudy. His *understudy*," she repeated as she poked Geraldine in her ample bosom.

"Don't act as though you weren't doing the same thing with Hal as I was," Celia snapped back. "You and Vivian made absolute fools of yourselves. Hal never wanted either one of you."

"Well, he certainly didn't want you, you two-bit tramp," Celia screamed. "You threatened him, and I heard it! You bullied me into keeping my mouth shut, but you're not going to bully me anymore!"

"That's enough!" Zane said as he stepped between the two women. "This is a wake! Celia, you are way out of line!"

"Nobody cares about what you think, *understudy*. You need to back off and shut up," Celia told him angrily.

"You can't talk to either one of us like that," Zane answered fiercely.

"Oh, just shut up and mind your own business," Geraldine told him with a snap. "This doesn't concern you, Zane."

He looked at her askance for a moment before he spoke. "But I was defending you!"

"I don't need *anyone* doing that, especially not you," Geraldine said with some sting in her voice. "I'm a grown woman, and I can take care of myself! Do you understand that?"

He held his palms up and retreated a bit, but from the expression on his face, it was pretty clear to me that particular romance was at its end.

I thought the fireworks were over, but I didn't count on Karen Lexington showing up for the wake a minute later.

She walked up the aisle and mounted the stage in silence. Wearing black again—this time from her shoes to the veil perched on her head—she looked every bit the part of a mourner ripped from an old movie. As she reached the group, she lifted the veil, and then she started in on them. I didn't know if she'd missed the earlier fireworks or if she'd been waiting in the shadows behind us in order to make a more dramatic entrance.

"I see Hillary and Vivian are both too good to mourn the loss of my dearly beloved," she said icily. "We don't need them here, anyway. Vivian came in last place in the race for Hal's affections, and Hillary has lived more in her fantasy world than she ever did in reality. She acts mousy, but deep inside, she yearns to be the bride at every wedding and the corpse at every funeral. I say good riddance to them both."

"That's not a very nice thing to say," Max told her.

"Oh, I've got worse coming, and you're all going to stand there and take it. Besides, I won't take etiquette lessons from a has-been TV commercial actor who only *thinks* he's a director," she snapped at him. "Everyone knows that it's *your* fault my Hal is dead, even if no one else has the courage to say it out loud."

"I didn't kill the man," Max said angrily.

"You are wrong, sir. You and your stupid little gimmicky ten seconds of darkness made it possible. You might as well have plunged the blade into his heart yourself."

The words clearly stung Max into silence, something I never would have dreamed was even possible. I knew that she had just voiced what he'd been thinking himself all along, and it left the man in some kind of comatose state.

"Have you been drinking, Karen?" Zane asked her coolly.

"What if I have?" she countered as she turned her attention to him. "You wannabe womanizer. You must be so proud of yourself, convincing two old women to fall for you, all the while you were stabbing Hal in the back. *He* knew you were the one who spread those rumors about him and nearly ruined his reputation."

"What rumors are you talking about?" Zane countered.

"Don't act so innocent. You claimed that he was stealing from the collection plate at church, and they asked him to leave, just in case it was true," she said. I hadn't heard that story, and no one else had mentioned it in the course of our investigation either. Had we missed out on a big clue somewhere along the line?

"That was twenty-five years ago!" Zane shouted. Almost as an afterthought, he added, "And besides, it wasn't me."

"We all know better than that, you Judas," she said icily.

"Even if I did what you claim, I wasn't anywhere near him when he died!" Zane protested.

"He didn't just die! He was murdered!" she shouted at him.

That just left Celia and Geraldine. "Don't think I've left you two out," she said after she managed to calm herself down.

Geraldine said loftily, "Nobody cares what you think, Karen. We're willing to cut you a bit of slack, but you've worn out your welcome here. Go home and sleep it off."

It was an interesting approach; I had to give her that. Who in her right mind would poke that particular bear at that moment in time?

"At least *I* can sober up. Your soul is so poisonous you're going to die of cancer from it eating you up," Karen said with such vindictiveness that I shuddered in my seat. I hadn't heard something so wicked spoken out loud for a very long time. "You probably didn't have the guts to kill him," she said dismissively. "You just tried to replace him with a poor copy."

"Zane wasn't a copy of anyone!" she protested. "Now that Hillary knows about us, I can say it out loud. Zane and I were off in the wings together, sharing a private moment, during Max's little blackout. Isn't that right, Zane?"

It was clear that the understudy didn't want to acknowledge it, but Zane finally spoke. "It's true enough, though I'm ashamed to admit it now." He stared hard at Geraldine for a few seconds before he added, "You and I are through. Don't bother coming by my house tonight. I'm done with your nonsense."

"You're just upset. We all are," Geraldine said, trying to cajole him a bit.

"Why should we believe either one of you?" Karen asked haughtily. "For all I know, you did it together, and now you're giving each other alibis."

"Nevertheless, it's still the truth," he said with a sigh.

Celia wasn't going to wait for her salvo from Karen. She stormed off the stage as the mourning woman took aim at her. "Where do you think you're going?"

"Away from you," Celia said angrily. "Don't try to stop me."

"If I were going to do that, you would be stopped, just like you stopped Hal," she said, pointing a finger at the actress as though she were the Grim Reaper herself.

"What are you talking about?" Celia asked haltingly. "What do you *think* you know, Karen?"

"I'll share that with the police, and then everyone will know," Karen told her triumphantly.

"There's nothing to share," Celia said, but she started moving so quickly that it caught us all off guard. As she headed for the exit, Darby decided to make his presence known from behind the group and as far away from Celia as he could be.

"What do you need to tell me, Karen?" Darby asked as the place erupted. Usually the chief of police was a more calming influence, but not in the face of this mob.

"What are you doing here, spying on us?" Zane snapped out, clearly wanting to focus his anger on someone who wasn't intent on destroying him.

"You're not welcome here, Darby Jones," Geraldine agreed, taking her former boyfriend's side. "Does your mother know you're lurking in the shadows like some kind of twisted pervert?"

As they all started accosting Darby, Grace poked me as she stood. "Let's go after her," she said as she pointed to Celia, just vanishing through the lobby doors behind us.

I stood and followed her as well. Why had we both just sat there so calmly while Celia was making her escape? I suppose it was because we were mesmerized by what Karen Lexington would do next, but that was no excuse. As honorary and unofficial officers of the law, we'd failed our volunteer posts miserably, but maybe there was still time for us to redeem ourselves.

No such luck.

By the time we got outside, Celia Laslow was long gone.

We made our way back inside to see just what kind of incriminating evidence Karen might have had on the actress and whether her accusation was spot on or if it was just a way of tweaking a past rival for her late boyfriend's affections.

"Karen, you need to come with me," Darby said as he put a hand on her shoulder.

"I'm not finished here yet," she said, slurring her words for the first time. After looking around the room, she added, "Then again, maybe I am. You're all nothing but traitors, cowards, and fools." Before she left, though, she stared right through Max and said, "I'm withdrawing from your little theater group. There's a stench about it that offends me." She then turned to Darby with a triumphant smile and added, "I'm ready now."

Once they were gone, there wasn't much left for the rest of us to do. Wounds had been opened, bandages had been ripped off, and so many accusations had been slung around that no one was in the mood to send Hal off anymore.

As Grace and I approached the treat table, Geraldine accosted me. "We didn't do it, Suzanne! I don't care what that vile woman said. Why would we? What possible motive would we have had? We'd already found each other!"

"Maybe Hal spurned you again, or maybe one of you wanted the role to be Zane's," I said as I gathered up the boxes of donuts that were left. As I'd suspected, I'd made way too many of them. "There could be motives for either one of you killing him that we haven't even uncovered yet."

"I would never do such a thing to get a part," Zane snapped beside her. "The truth is that Geraldine didn't do it, and neither did I. I don't know who did, but it wasn't us. Believe what you want to believe, but we were together when it happened." He walked over to Max. "It probably goes without saying, but I'm out too. Acting has lost its appeal to me."

As Zane started for the door, Geraldine followed. "Wait for me, love," she called out cloyingly.

He just sped up his pace, and I had to wonder if he was going looking for Hillary after what had happened onstage earlier.

I wasn't sure the wardrobe supervisor would be getting the good deal she had hoped for if he succeeded in his quest.

"Are they telling the truth?" Grace asked me as we watched them leave.

"I don't have anything to back it up, but something in my gut tells me they are," I said. "I don't know if it's their body language or what, but I almost think Zane would have rather given up his alibi than help her out."

"Well, when it comes down to it, I *always* go with your gut until it's proven wrong," she said. Now it was just Grace, Max, and me left.

"Are you okay?" I asked him.

He seemed to be coming out of it. "I've been called worse, but not by much," he joked, trying to smile his way out of the memory of what had happened, but I could tell that he'd been hurt by Karen's brief but savage attack.

"Don't pay any attention to her. She doesn't know what she's talking about," I told him as I patted his arm. "Do you want some donuts to take home to Emily?"

"No, thanks," he said as he looked around the stage. "I guess I'd better clean this mess up."

I looked myself and saw that it wasn't that bad. "Go home to your wife. Grace and I will handle this."

"I'm not even going to fight you on it," he said with a sigh. "Thank you."

"You're welcome," I answered, and then he was gone.

"Did you really just draft me for your little impromptu cleanup committee?" Grace asked me with a wry smile.

"It's not too bad. Besides, you were the one who volunteered my services to provide the donuts for this little get-together in the first place, remember?"

"That's true," Grace said as she started throwing used plates, cups, and napkins into a trashcan off to the side. "How about this booze? Do we at least get to keep that?"

At that moment, Max poked his head back in through the doorway. "Just put the hooch in my office in back. Well, it's more of a cupboard really, but it's all mine."

"There goes that fringe benefit," Grace said as she did as Max had asked. "Now what are we going to do with all of these donuts?"

I looked at them with such distaste that I couldn't stand the sight of them anymore. They were poisoned with all of the pain and suffering that had been flung around on that stage, and I didn't want to have anything to do with them.

"Throw them away," I said grimly.

"What?"

"You heard me, Grace. Get rid of them."

"*All* of them?" she asked me gently.

"Every last one," I ordered, and she did exactly as I'd asked.

Maybe we couldn't destroy the bad blood that had come forth during what was supposed to have been a wake, but we could at least get rid of every last bit of evidence of it.

Chapter 19

"WHAT SHOULD WE DO WITH the leftover donuts in the back of the Jeep?" Grace asked me cautiously. I was in a mood, and she knew it.

"Throw them out too," I said.

"Come on, Suzanne. That's not like you. What did these delicious little treats do to you?"

"Would you like them?" I asked her.

"Don't tempt me," she replied.

I thought about it, and then I came up with an idea. "Let's go see if Paige wants any more."

"That's an excellent idea," Grace said.

We parked in front of Donut Hearts on our way home and grabbed the three boxes we had left. "Knock, knock," I said as I opened the door to The Last Page. I loved having the bookstore across the street from my shop, and even more, it was wonderful having Paige in April Springs. I decided to put the wake behind me right then and there, and I tried to put on a smile. "Donuts, anyone?"

"That's wonderful," Paige said as she gladly took them.

I spotted a new sign above the table where Paige hosted authors on tour sometimes. "Who's Desmond Wilson?" I asked her.

"He's someone new," she admitted and then added softly, "Not really my cup of tea, but I couldn't say no. His publicist was so adamant about allowing him to sign here."

"What's he write?" Grace asked as I picked up one of the garish covers. The hardback sported a fanged demon covered in more blood than even a ghoul should be sporting.

"It's a new series about a vampire serial killer," Paige said with a shiver. "I can't imagine what kind of customers we're going to be getting here tonight. Would you ladies like to come and hear him talk?"

"Thanks for the offer," I said quickly, "but the bounds of friendship only go so far. I like a good cozy mystery where the violence happens offstage."

"Grace?" she asked hopefully.

"That's a hard pass," my friend said without even trying to hide her feelings about the book's theme.

"I understand. You can't blame me for trying, can you?"

"Well, maybe a little bit," I said teasingly as I dropped the book back onto the stack. "How many did you bring in for this event?"

"Two cases," she admitted.

"Don't you think that might be a hard sell for April Springs?" I asked her.

Lowering her voice, she said, "What could I do? He promised to buy whatever's left at full retail."

"I'm beginning to see why you were so willing to host him," I said.

Paige shrugged. "I do what I have to do to stay afloat. The book's really not half bad. I took one home last night and read the first few chapters."

Grace looked at her askance. "Are you telling us that you read a book about vampire serial killers before *bed*?"

"Technically, there's only *one* vampire serial killer in the book," Paige said.

"Isn't one enough?" Grace asked.

"It is in my book," I said as I headed for the door. "Good luck."

"Thanks. I might have to get Darby to provide security for the event," she said with a frown.

"Try Rick Handler. He's been known to moonlight every now and then," I told her.

"As a security guard?" she asked.

"You'll have to ask him about that," I told her. If Rick was willing to decorate sets in his spare time, I couldn't imagine him having a problem acting as security for one of Paige's bookstore events.

"I may have to," she admitted.

Back in the Jeep, it was a quick drive to Grace's place. "Want to come in?" she offered.

"I'd better not," I said. "I apologize."

"What for?"

"We both know that I'm in a wretched mood. Maybe a nap and a shower will make me right again," I told her.

"That's asking an awful lot from a couch and a bit of water," she answered, smiling at me.

"Hey, they've been known to perform miracles before."

"At least stay for a second, Suzanne," Grace said. "I've got some sweet tea, and we can sit out here on the porch. I'd like to discuss what we saw this afternoon, and I'm afraid if we wait too long, I'll forget something important."

"Something *did* happen, didn't it?" I asked her.

"I'd say a *lot* happened," Grace replied.

"I don't mean that. I feel as though we were handed a clue today, an important one at that, but I can't seem to put my finger on what it was."

"That's all the more reason for us to discuss it then," she said.

"Okay, but just for a few minutes," I replied.

"I'll be right back with our drinks."

My hostess was as good as her word, and after she handed me a glass of sweet tea, I took a healthy sip. "Just the right amount of sugar," I told her.

"Do you mean enough to chew?" Grace asked with a grin.

"Just about."

"So, where do things stand now?" Grace asked me.

"Well, I know that I might be wrong, but I'm inclined to put Geraldine and Zane on the back burner, if not off the stove entirely," I admitted.

"So, you really did buy their alibi."

"I did, only because neither one of them seemed all that eager to provide it," I said.

"There's no easy way to verify it, is there, though?" Grace asked me.

"No, but Celia shot out of there like a rocket when Karen said that she had something incriminating against her."

Grace responded, "Actually, what she said was that Celia had stopped Hal somehow. That's not the same as killing him."

"Maybe not, but if that were the case, why did she bolt?" I asked.

"To be fair, Celia wasn't the only one. Hillary could have set an indoor record for the hundred-yard dash the way she tore out of there so quickly."

"At least she had a reason," I said. "It couldn't have been easy seeing the man she thought she was in love with be with another woman."

"I doubt she would have kept thinking that if she'd hung around," Grace said. "Geraldine and Zane are over; there's no doubt about that in my mind."

"Mine, either, which makes them alibiing each other that much stronger. If Zane could have thrown her under the bus, I'm pretty sure he would have, even if it meant jeopardizing his own alibi."

"So, that leaves us with Celia, doesn't it?" Grace asked.

"I'd have to say so. I'd love to know what Karen told Darby about her," I said. "Or even where Celia is at the moment. Do you think they have an all-points bulletin out on her?"

"It wouldn't surprise me in the least," Grace said. "I wish our guys would come home."

"Darby seems to have things in hand," I answered in his defense.

"Oh, he's doing the police work just fine. I just miss Stephen, and I know you miss Jake."

"Shoot, I even miss Phillip a little, but don't tell him I said that," I told her.

"I won't."

I finished my tea and then stood as I said, "If you don't mind, I'm going to take that shower now and grab a nap too. Today has been exhausting, and not just because Emma and I made twice as many donuts as we usually do and skipped our break altogether."

"Absolutely," Grace said as she stood with me. "Would you like to grab a bite tonight? I've been craving Napoli's since our near-miss last night."

"That sounds great to me," I said. "I can even stay up past my bedtime, since Emma and Sharon are running Donut Hearts tomorrow."

"Woohoo," Grace answered with a grin. "It's Ladies' Night."

"Let's not get *too* excited," I said with a smile of my own. "After all, I still have to get to bed pretty early."

"Don't worry about that. I'll make sure you're back at a reasonable hour."

"Then it's a deal," I said, and then I drove home to my empty cottage. Part of the reason I was in such a bad place was because of the murder and how Hal's memory had been sullied by that wake and everyone's behavior at it, but I knew that some of it was due to the fact that I was lonely. I missed Jake when he was gone, and I found myself hoping that he'd come back home soon so I could show him just how much.

It was great being able to take a hot shower again, and I would have to thank Momma for making it happen so quickly. My mood improved a bit, and after I got dressed, I lay down on the couch in the living room and tried to make my mind go blank, something that was tough to do given what had happened so very recently. I just knew that a vital clue was dancing somewhere in the back of my thoughts, but I couldn't for the life of me put my finger on it.

It didn't come as a great surprise to me that my sleep wasn't a restful one. In it, I found myself hovering above stage the night of the dress rehearsal, watching the cast and crew getting ready for the show. As my projected spirit looked around, I saw that Hal was already seated in his chair on stage, Geraldine and Zane were off in the wings, making out, and Vivian was no doubt outside having her cigarette break. I hadn't had a chance to spot Max, Celia, or Hillary yet when the lights on stage suddenly went out. My dream self was plunged into darkness as much as the cast and crew had been the night of the murder, but I could see a little bit of something, an outline here and there.

When I glanced at Hal, I saw that he wasn't alone.

Someone was standing over him, and just as suddenly as the lights had been extinguished, they plunged the blade into Hal Embry's chest.

At that instant, I saw a flash of light coming off the blade as though it was Hal's spirit leaving his body. It projected illumination for barely an instant, but it was still long enough for me to see who had killed him.

In my dream, Hillary Teal was standing over the dying man, one hand on the hilt of the knife while the other covered his mouth to keep him from crying out.

I woke up in a cold sweat, wondering why I had just experienced such a vivid dream and trying to figure out if it had been based on something in reality or something I'd seen or heard and had just missed. Then I realized that maybe the reason Hillary hadn't wanted to go to the wake hadn't had anything to do with Zane and Geraldine. Maybe she couldn't bring herself to do it because of her guilty conscience. Had she been about to confess to Grace and me earlier? She might have been, but then she stopped herself and tried to blame Celia for the murder instead. Then later at the theater, she'd looked panicked when I'd told her to stop fleeing the wake. I'd told her that I had something I needed to talk to her about, and her face had gone white as a sheet. What had she suspected? I didn't have a great deal of evidence against her, but I was determined to double my efforts investigating her. My gut hadn't failed me yet, and it was telling me that Hillary was the one we should all be looking at, not Celia or anyone else who'd been there on stage when the murder had occurred.

And then I realized what I'd forgotten. The very first time Grace and I had spoken to Hillary, she'd said that she'd been working on Vivian's costume just before the murder occurred, but we learned later that Vivian had been outside, sneaking a cigarette. Hillary's alibi had crumbled, but I hadn't even noticed! How had we missed that? We had something to turn over to Darby now, something that cracked the case wide open. I had a feeling we'd learn why she'd done it once she was confronted with reality.

And that was when I heard someone pounding on the front door of the cottage.

I looked out the window and saw that it was Hillary Teal.

She wasn't alone though.

Grace was standing there in front of her, and there was a knife to her throat.

"Open the door, Suzanne, or I'll kill her right here in front of you," Hillary said shakily.

Chapter 20

"THERE'S NO NEED FOR that," I told Hillary calmly as I opened the door and let them both in.

"Suzanne, what is she talking about? What is happening here?" Grace asked me. Her voice was on the edge of hysteria, and I couldn't blame her. After all, she had a knife to her throat, not something that ordinarily inspired calm, rational behavior.

"It's going to be okay, Grace," I said.

"I don't see how," she answered. She tried to turn to talk to Hillary, but the older woman pressed the knife a bit harder and drew a line of blood on Grace's neck. "Why are you doing this?"

Hillary looked at me knowingly. "Ask your partner. She knows."

I could try to bluff her and hope that we could make her see reason, but one look into her eyes told me that reason had long left her. The costumer must have seen something in my gaze. "Tell her, or she dies," Hillary said wearily. "At this point, I have nothing to lose."

"You knew more than we gave you credit for, and you knew it sooner than you admitted," I said.

Hillary looked pleased by my statement. "Nobody ever notices the crew on these productions. It was almost as though I wasn't even there."

"Would someone *please* explain it to me?" Grace asked, the desperation creeping into her voice.

"Go ahead, Suzanne. Enlighten her."

I took a deep breath, and then I laid it all out in the open. "Hillary knew about the affair between Zane and Geraldine *before* the dress rehearsal, though she didn't admit it to us. You did a fine job acting, by the way. You should have been onstage yourself."

"I tried out once, but Max said that I was too valuable working as the costume supervisor. Hah. I was a glorified seamstress when I should have been onstage."

"You also learned that Zane was going on for Hal, and the opening scene with the knife must have made you realize that was your chance to get your revenge for him choosing someone else. You never knew Hal finally made it at the last second and they switched places, did you? Hal Embry was *never* your intended victim, was he?"

"Of course he wasn't! I didn't find out what I'd done until Max brought the lights back up. No one else noticed that Hal was dead, but I nearly fainted dead away when I saw that he was dead and not Zane. I managed to hold it together though, and no one saw that I was shaken up. As I said, I was invisible."

"So you used that to your advantage," I said.

"You're just figuring some of this out, aren't you?" Hillary asked a bit hesitantly.

"I had no idea you were the killer until it came to me in a dream on my couch a few minutes ago. What gave you away was when I finally realized that your alibi of working on Vivian's costume was a lie. She was outside, smoking a cigarette, so you *couldn't* have been working on her wardrobe. When we interrupted you at Zane's earlier, you were there to finish the job, weren't you?" I asked her. What could the truth hurt now?

"Yes, it's all true, but if you didn't know I'd done it until just now, then what was that all about at the auditorium today?" she asked haltingly.

"I was just trying to help. I wanted you to be brave and face reality," I told her. "I was bluffing, Hillary, but I didn't want you to do something you would regret for the rest of your life."

"It's a bit too late for that," she said, real tears starting to fall now as her world collapsed around her.

"It's *never* too late," I said. "You didn't mean to kill Hal, and you don't have to kill us."

"What choice do I have? My life is over," she said, the hand holding the knife growing white with the tenseness of her grip.

"It doesn't have to be," I said. "Put the knife down. We'll help you get through this."

Hillary Teal's hand wavered for a moment, and I thought I might be able to talk her down. But it was touch and go, and I couldn't be sure she wouldn't change her mind at the last second as she had when she'd come so close to confessing her crime to us before.

Grace must have felt the pressure ease on her neck. In an instant, she struck out at the killer's hand as she dropped to the floor and scrambled over toward me before the killer could recover. Hillary shifted the knife in her hand as I reached for a nearby lamp. It wasn't much, but at least it was something I could use to defend us from that blade.

If Hillary came at us again, I would be ready for her.

What she did next surprised us though.

Instead of trying to stab Grace or even me, Hillary reversed the knife handle and plunged the blade straight into her own chest.

It was ironic that she'd used the same kind of weapon in the same manner on herself this time instead of on someone else.

Chapter 21

"GRACE, CALL 911," I shouted as I knelt down beside Hillary. I checked for a pulse at her throat, and there was one there, though thready at best.

"It hurts so much," Hillary said as she clutched at the knife and tried to pull it out.

I stopped her hand. "Don't move it! It might be the only thing keeping you alive."

"I don't deserve to live," she said, sobbing from the pain and the anguish of what she'd done, both to Hal and now herself.

"That's too bad, because I'm not going to let you throw your life away, no matter what you've done," I said as I heard an ambulance in the background. It must have been close by, which was a good thing. Hillary hadn't lost a great deal of blood yet, but I had a hunch that knife was acting as a dam, holding it all in. If it was removed, or even shifted in its place, I doubted that she'd have long to live, and I wasn't going to let that happen if I could help it. I knew that she'd killed a man, and she deserved to be punished for it, but that didn't mean that I could just stand by and watch her take the coward's way out by killing herself right in front of me.

To Grace's credit, even though she'd been the one in the most mortal danger, she knelt beside me with a towel and tried to apply pressure with me.

As Hillary lay there, she whispered. "I'm sorry. For everything. Please forgive me."

And then Hillary's eyes closed, and I was afraid that we'd lost another battle even as the ambulance pulled up to the cottage's front door.

Chapter 22

AN HOUR LATER, GRACE and I were going over what had happened with Hillary for the fourth time at the police station when Darby got a phone call. "Sorry, but I've got to take this," he said. After a few moments of mostly listening, he hung up and looked at us intently. "I'm sorry, ladies, but they weren't able to save her. Hillary's gone."

It took a second for it to sink in, though I suspected that Hillary Teal had lost her will to live *before* she'd plunged that knife into her own chest. She'd taken Hal's life, mistaking him for a scorned lover that never was, and she'd paid the ultimate price for it. *None* of it had to happen, but there was nothing anyone could do about it now. Hal was gone, and so was Hillary. I didn't go in for the poetic justice of her using the same method of murder on herself as she had on her victim, but I was sure that others would when they found out what had really happened.

"Are we finished here?" I asked Darby absently. "When it comes right down to it, we really don't know all that much."

"You knew enough to solve the case. That's more than I can say," he admitted sadly. The investigation had aged him somehow, as though the loss of life had registered on him directly, and I was certain that he would be eager for the real chief of police to come back home.

Grace, Momma, and I all had good reasons of our own to want that men's getaway to be over.

We had all been lucky enough to find people to love, people who loved us right back.

It was something that Hillary would never know now.

"Can I give you a ride home?" Darby asked.

I shuddered at the very thought of it. Would I *ever* be able to go back to that cottage again after seeing a woman kill herself right in front of me? It might happen someday, but I knew that it wouldn't be anytime soon.

"That's okay. We'll walk," Grace said as she took my hand and pulled me out of the chair.

Once we were outside in the sun, not even its direct warmth could take the chill from me.

"Grace, I can't go back there," I said softly, my voice now barely above a whisper.

"That's okay. You don't have to. You can stay with me, but if that's still too close, I'm sure your mother would love to have you stay with her." She squeezed my hand again. "Suzanne, we *all* love you. You'll have a roof over your head as long as any one of us does."

"Thank you," I said. "For everything."

"Hey, that's what friends are for," she answered. "Now let's try to move forward and put this all behind us. What do you say?"

"All I can do is try."

"That's always good enough for me, and for everyone else too," she said.

And then, with the next step I took, I tried to take her advice and forget what had just happened.

It would take some real work, but I could do it.

After all, I wouldn't be doing it alone, and that made all the difference in the world.

RECIPES

Lovely Apple Fritter Balls

I've been a fan of apple fritters for as long as I can remember. There's something about them that just makes my mouth water at the very thought of them. I nearly always make them with chopped apples inside, but once in a blue moon, I fill them with apple pie filling instead. They are nearly as good as the original while providing a nice change of pace, not that these fritters need one, in my opinion! My shape is different from the conventional fritter, but they're easy to make, and I'm usually in a hurry to start eating these!

Ingredients

Dry

3⁄4 cup all-purpose unbleached white flour

1 tablespoon baking powder

1 tablespoon cinnamon

1⁄4 teaspoon salt

Wet

1⁄3 cup milk (whole milk is best, but 2% will work just fine)

1⁄4 cup granulated sugar

1 egg, beaten

1⁄2 cup chopped apple (something tart; I like Granny Smiths for this)

DIRECTIONS

Heat enough vegetable oil for frying to 360° on your stovetop while you mix the batter. While the oil is coming up to temperature, sift the flour, baking powder, cinnamon, and salt together then stir in the milk, sugar, and beaten egg. Fold in the chopped apple pieces, and then take a teaspoon of batter and rake it into the fryer with another spoon. If the dough doesn't rise soon, gently nudge it with a chopstick, being careful not to splatter oil. After 2 minutes, check and then flip, frying for another minute on the other side. These times may vary given too many factors to count, so keep a close eye on the fritters.

Makes about a dozen small fritter balls.

Momma's Best Pot Roast

I make my pot roast just like Momma does in the book, using a slow cooker to let the meat and vegetables come together slowly over low heat. The smells alone coming from this dish fill the house with such a lovely aroma that it's almost worth making this dish as a room freshener! One of the best things about this is the low cost. If you watch for sales, you can find decent cuts of meat that won't break your budget.

The results have never failed to please me and my family.

Ingredients

2 tablespoons canola oil

2 tablespoons all-purpose unbleached white flour

1/8 teaspoon salt

1/8 teaspoon pepper

1 boneless beef chuck roast, 2 to 2 1/2 pounds

2 medium russet or red potatoes, peeled and cubed

carrots, baby or peeled, cut into 1-inch sections, about 1 lb.

Any good onion soup mix packet, about 1 oz.

1 cup tap water

1 tablespoon of either cornstarch, all-purpose flour, or powdered tapioca

1/3 cup cold water

Directions

Browning the meat before putting it in the crockpot is optional, but it's a step I always take. Using a burner set to medium on the stovetop, add the canola oil to a nonstick frying pan and warm it until a drop of water sizzles when dropped into it. While waiting, mix the flour, salt, and pepper together and then coat the roast with the mix. Brown the meat on all sides in the hot pan and then drain off the fat. In the slow cooker, spray the pot with nonstick vegetable spray (or use a slow-cooker liner, which makes cleanup super easy), and then add the potatoes and carrots to the bottom of the slow cooker. Add the browned roast next, and then sprinkle the soup mix on top. Next, add the water until the veggies are almost covered but not the roast.

Put the lid on the slow cooker and cook on HIGH for 6 hours, or until the roast falls apart with gentle prodding from a fork. Remove the roast and veggies to a serving plate and cover everything with aluminum foil to keep it all warm then strain the liquid and pour it into the pan you used to brown the meat originally. In a small bowl, add the thickening agent (cornstarch, all-purpose flour, or powdered tapioca) to the cold water and then stir it all together in the pan, heating it at a simmer until the gravy is finished to your liking. Serve the gravy directly on the roast and carrots if you'd like or offer it separately. If you want to skip making the gravy, the meal's just fine without it! Either way, it should be delicious!

Serves 4 to 6 people, depending on serving size.

Baked Lemon Donuts

I go through phases where only a lemon-flavored donut will do, so
I've got a variety of donuts I like to make when I have that particular
craving. Usually, I make my treats with my family in mind, but sometimes, I find that it's okay to be selfish, especially when it comes to
donuts! These baked donuts are particularly light if done right, but be
warned. To some folks, the lemon flavoring is a bit overwhelming, so
make and serve these at your own risk! They are great iced with a lemon
glaze (using lemon juice instead of water in your icing mix) or dusted
with powdered sugar.

Ingredients

1/2 cup half and half (whole milk, 2%, or even 1% can be substituted)

2 tablespoons unsalted butter, melted

2 tablespoons granulated sugar

1 tablespoon lemon juice

2 teaspoons lemon zest

1 teaspoon vanilla extract (lemon extract could be substituted)

1/2 vanilla bean, scraped

1 cup ready-made pancake mix (I use Bisquick, but any mix will do)

Directions

Preheat the oven to 375°F.

While waiting for the oven to come to temperature, take a medi-
um-sized bowl and mix the half and half, melted butter, sugar, lemon

juice, lemon zest, vanilla extract, and the scraped vanilla bean seeds together, reserving the pancake mix for last. Once the wet ingredients are incorporated, add the pancake mix and blend it all together until mostly combined, being careful not to overmix, as this could cause denser donuts.

Use donut shaped or regular muffin pans and add the mixture three-quarters of the way up the sides.

Bake 5 to 8 minutes or until an inserted toothpick comes out clean, then remove the donuts to a cooling rack and dust immediately with powdered confectioners' sugar or glaze.

Yields 10 to 12 donuts.

If you enjoy Jessica Beck Mysteries and you would like to be notified when the next book is being released, please visit our website at jessicabeckmysteries.net for valuable information about Jessica's books, and sign up for her new-releases-only mail blast.

Your email address will not be shared, sold, bartered, traded, broadcast, or disclosed in any way. There will be no spam from us, just a friendly reminder when the latest book is being released, and of course, you can drop out at any time.

Other Books by Jessica Beck

The Donut Mysteries
Glazed Murder
Fatally Frosted
Sinister Sprinkles
Evil Éclairs
Tragic Toppings
Killer Crullers
Drop Dead Chocolate
Powdered Peril
Illegally Iced
Deadly Donuts
Assault and Batter
Sweet Suspects
Deep Fried Homicide
Custard Crime
Lemon Larceny
Bad Bites
Old Fashioned Crooks
Dangerous Dough
Troubled Treats
Sugar Coated Sins
Criminal Crumbs
Vanilla Vices
Raspberry Revenge
Fugitive Filling
Devil's Food Defense
Pumpkin Pleas
Floured Felonies
Mixed Malice

Tasty Trials
Baked Books
Cranberry Crimes
Boston Cream Bribes
Cherry Filled Charges
Scary Sweets
Cocoa Crush
Pastry Penalties
Apple Stuffed Alibies
Perjury Proof
Caramel Canvas
Dark Drizzles
Counterfeit Confections
Measured Mayhem
Blended Bribes
Sifted Sentences
Dusted Discoveries
Nasty Knead
Rigged Rising
Donut Despair
Whisked Warnings
Baker's Burden
Battered Bluff
The Hole Truth
Donut Disturb
The Classic Diner Mysteries
A Chili Death
A Deadly Beef
A Killer Cake
A Baked Ham
A Bad Egg
A Real Pickle

DONUT DISTURB** 181

A Burned Biscuit
The Ghost Cat Cozy Mysteries
Ghost Cat: Midnight Paws
Ghost Cat 2: Bid for Midnight
The Cast Iron Cooking Mysteries
Cast Iron Will
Cast Iron Conviction
Cast Iron Alibi
Cast Iron Motive
Cast Iron Suspicion
Nonfiction
The Donut Mysteries Cookbook

Made in the USA
Monee, IL
29 July 2021

74545682R00105